For Alex for always pushing me.
For Tiffany for never letting me get away with anything
And M, you told me to write it. So I did.

Chapter 1

The music was relentless through the mansion, the bass bouncing off of the floors and ceilings. Guests laughed and danced, their clothes grabbing every fashion trend since the eighties. Every corner of the grand hall was filled with conversation, blending into the music that echoed off walls adorned with art and intricate moldings. Floral arrangements filled the air with their rich fragrance, mingling with the scent of expensive perfumes.

James stood by the ornate mahogany bar, nursing a whiskey that had long lost its chill, eyes narrowed in irritation at the spectacle unfolding around him. His posture rigid, but beneath the polished surface, was raged unchecked. James despised the facade, hated pretending, He hated the superficial smiles and fake laughs.

Across the room, Leena moved effortlessly, radiant and captivating as always. Her laughter rang out, her smile, pulling everyone into her orbit. She wore a gown that accented her figure perfectly, accentuating her every move. James watched her from afar, bitterness festering beneath his carefully composed exterior. Every playful smile she cast toward other men felt intentional, deliberate wounds designed to punish him for his betrayal.

James raised his glass, taking another sip of his whiskey, wincing as

it burned down his throat. He recognized the game Leena's calcu-
lated revenge, a carefully choreographed act meant to humiliate
him publicly. She touched the shoulder of one guy, laughed softly
at a lawyers whispered joke, and leaned in slightly towards a young
entrepreneur, her eyes sparkling. Each action was precise, calculat-
ed, and devastatingly effective.

"You need to relax," a voice purred beside him. James turned,
finding Sophia, Leena's best friend, watching him with a mixture of
amusement and disdain. She was dressed like she was on the hunt,
dark curls cascading down her shoulders, her makeup flawless. She
raised an eyebrow, a smile tugging at the corners of her mouth.
"This is supposed to be fun" she said.

"Define fun," James scoffed, setting his glass down a lot harder than
intended, the sound jarring through the party's noise. "Acting like
it's OK? Watching Leena flirt with every guy here?"

Sophia's smile faltered slightly, replaced by an expression of re-
strained sympathy. "You did this to yourself, James. Consequences.
You know?"

James stiffened, guilt surging briefly before being replaced by defen-
sive anger. "Don't act like you understand, you have her side. Still i
don't think you know half of it."

Sophia sighed softly, her eyes momentarily softening. "Maybe I
don't fully understand, James. But I do know how deeply she's hurting. And you need to realize that your ego isn't the only thing that
matters here."

Unable to bear Sophia's gaze any longer, James pushed away from
the bar, leaving her standing there, a thoughtful expression etched
onto her face. He moved through the crowd mechanically, smiling
politely when required, exchanging superficial pleasantries, each
interaction felt increasingly hollow.

Finally reaching the doors that led out to the expansive balcony, James pushed through them, welcoming the cool night air. The sudden chill cleared his head momentarily, allowing regret to seep back in. Gripping the railing until his knuckles turned white, he stared out over the city skyline below, feeling isolated and deeply alone.

His mind inevitably drifted back, memories flooding in, each more painful and vivid than the last. It had begun quietly, the slow, relentless erosion of affection and intimacy. Leena had always been vibrant, strong, and passionate, but the stress and exhaustion had worn her down. James had felt she pushed him away or failed to see it, maybe he'd simply chosen not to.

He remembered specific arguments vividly, the anger in Leena's voice when she found him working late, neglecting her. Each instance had seemed minor at the time, small irritations easily dismissed. But they had accumulated steadily, forming an impenetrable barrier between them.

James recalled clearly the night he had crossed line, seeking comfort elsewhere. Loneliness and emotional isolation and a lot of alcohol had driven him into the arms of someone else, a betrayal he nor Leena could forgive or move past easily. His regret was immediate, overwhelming, but by then the damage had already been done.

A soft rustle behind him snapped James back. He turned swiftly, his body tensed defensively, only to find Leena standing quietly, framed beautifully by the glow from the mansion's interior. Her defiant eyes appeared weary, shadowed by unspoken sorrow.

"Are you done throwing it in my face?" He asked quietly, bitterness in every word.

Leena's smile was sad, resigned. She stepped closer, joining him at the railing, her eyes fixed on the distant lights. "Funny, James. I was just about to ask you that."

The silence between them was thick with unspoken regrets and unresolved grievances. Eventually, Leena sighed softly, her voice barely audible over the distant hum of laughter and music from inside the mansion. "I'm tired, tired of all of it."

James felt his anger begin to go away, replaced by a weariness that mirrored hers. "Me too," he whispered, barely trusting his voice.

Their fragile peace was shattered as voices approached the balcony, other guests seeking fresh air. Leena quickly straightened, effortlessly slipping back into her composed social persona.

"Enjoy the rest of the night," she murmured coolly, her mask of indifference slipping seamlessly back into place as she retreated into the warmth and light of the party.

James watched her disappear, his anger reignited by frustration, regret, and resentment. He stood alone once again, feeling the weight of his choices pressing heavily upon him. Below, the city sprawled silently, indifferent to the chaos, unaware that the evening was on the verge of spiraling out of control.

He lingered a few moments longer on the balcony, letting the night air cut through his thoughts before finally turning and walking back inside. The mansion was hot now, filled with expectation and judgment. Conversations seemed sharper, and it felt like all eyes were looking at him

Leena reappeared near the main staircase, gracefully accepting a glass of champagne from a server. Smiling effortlessly as an older gentleman in a suit whispered something that made her laugh too loud, too long, too over the top.

From across the room, Sophia caught James's eye again. Her expression had changed. She looked as though she wanted to intervene, but Leena was already pulling her aside. The two women disappeared down a hallway leading to one of the private side parlors.

In the room, Leena dropped the act. Her body slumped slightly as she leaned against the fireplace mantle.

"He's watching me like a ghost," she muttered.

Sophia crossed her arms. "Because you haunt him. Just like he haunts you."

Leena didn't respond. She stared into the fireplace
"I don't know what I'm doing," she finally said. "This dress, the flirting, the laughs I thought it would make me feel i don't know. In control. But it doesn't. I just feel you know tired."

Sophia stepped beside her and placed a hand gently on Leena's arm. "You don't need to punish yourself to punish him. You're allowed to want more than survival. You're allowed to want peace."

Leena gave her a smile. "I don't even know what peace looks like anymore."

They rejoined the party a few minutes later, with the masks readjusted. James saw them return, Leena now arm-in-arm with Sophia, the way women link elbows when they want to push away the world.

"Mr. Langston!" Someone called from the side.

James turned toward a group of his co-workers. Most were half-drunk, all wearing the kind of laughs that came from bonuses and self-importance. They greeted him with back-pats and jabs.

"Didn't think we'd see you tonight," one said, tipping a glass. "Wife hasn't killed you yet?"

James offered a smile. "Only socially."

Small chuckles. Then someone changed the subject.

Leena's laughter floated in again this time at a man James didn't recognize. Tall. Handsome. His hand lightly rested on the small of her back.

It was little, but it hit James. He excused himself from the group without explanation went towards her.

Leena caught his approach and tilted her head subtly, the corners of her mouth lifting. She turned to the man.

"This is my husband," she said evenly. "James."

The man extended a hand. "Julian."

James shook it, squeezing like it would snap. "Pleasure."

Julian excused himself. The air between James and Leena became razor-thin.

"You don't get to be like this" she said under her breath.

"I'm not," James lied. "Just curious how far you're willing to go."

She looked at him. "I didn't cheat. You did. I'm the one who slept in the same bed, alone, wondering what happened while you were out correcting your mistakes between someone else's thighs."

The music swelled. The chandelier above flickered.

"I know," James said. "You don't have to keep throwing it in my face over and over. I know."

Leena's mask slipped. For just a second, her eyes glistened.

"Then stop acting like you're the only one who lost something," she whispered.

And with that, she turned, disappearing again.

James remained rooted in place, not out of pride or anger but because if he moved, he feared the pieces would fall away.

And there'd be nothing left for him to hold onto.

Chapter 2

They drove in silence.

The sound of the turn signal click, click, click was the only thing keeping him to the present. Rain streaked across the windshield, smeared by the wipers into blurry streaks of light from the oncoming traffic. His knuckles were white against the steering wheel, and his jaw was locked so tight it was giving him a headache. Beside him, Leena stared out her window, her arms crossed, her silence deafening.

Neither of them had said a word since they left the party. The night still lingered and hung like humidity between them. The streets of the city, once beautiful and shimmering in the glow of high-rise windows, now seemed to shrink in on them like a tunnel.

"You didn't have to do that in front of everyone," James said at last, his voice low, and steady.

Leena's laugh was sharp and humorless. "I'm sorry did I ruin it for you? You seemed to be playing the victim so well."

James's fingers flexed on the steering wheel. "You think this is easy for me?"

"No, I think you're a pussy" she said. "You didn't fight for me. You didn't even notice until i started to disappear."

He looked at her for a second just a second too long. The car swerved slightly before he corrected it.

"I tried," he said. "I know I screwed up. I know I let everything fall apart. But I wasn't the only one! "

Leena turned her head, finally facing him. Her voice dropped to a near whisper. "You didn't. You replaced me."

He flinched.

Just before they reached the turn for their street, a car coming the opposite direction hydroplaned and veered into their lane only for a split second but James had to swerve sharply to avoid it. The tires screamed across the soaked pavement, and the jolt yanked both of them forward in their seats.

Leena's hand flew to the dashboard instinctively. Her breath caught in her throat.

"Jesus Christ!" She hissed.

"I saw it," he muttered, more to himself than her.

But his heart was racing. Adrenaline twisted in his stomach. A few more inches and it wouldn't have been a scare. It would have been over.

James let out a breath he hadn't realized he was holding. He was still clutching the wheel like he wasn't in control. Rain poured blurring out the world. The close call didn't bring them together it drove another wedge.

Leena turned her head slightly. "You used to be my safe place," she said flatly. "Now I'm just waiting for a crash"

James didn't know what to say to that. So he said the worst thing instead.

"Then why are you still here?"

Leena blinked slowly, like the question hadn't surprised her,
"Because I'm stubborn. I was hurt James"
James opened his mouth, closed it, and opened it again. Nothing
came out.

"I know that now."

She turned back to the window. "Well too late."

James gritted his teeth and focused on the road. Water pooled in
the low spots of the asphalt, and the rain beat a rhythm against the
windshield. Leena's voice, quiet but filled with poison, cut through
the cabin.

"You know what the worst part is? I used to check the time every
day just to count the hours until you came home. Now, I just count
the hours I don't have to see your face."

James didn't respond right away. He couldn't. The words hit harder
than they should have. He tightened his grip on the wheel, blinking
harder than necessary as cars moved past.

"I never asked for hatred," he said finally.

"No. You just earned it," she whispered, turning her face back toward the window.

"You act like I woke up one day and decided to break us. Like I
enjoyed any of it."

"You didn't break us all at once, James. You chipped away at us. Little things. I begged for scraps, and you made me feel like a burden."

His throat tightened. "And you think I don't live with that every day?"

"I think you just learned to live with it. I never did."

He couldn't argue. Not with that.

Their home, a colonial tucked into the side of a tree-lined street, emerged from the mist like a ghost. The headlights casting warped shadows across the driveway as James parked the car.

Leena opened her door before the car had fully stopped. She moved quickly, disappearing up the steps and into the house without a second thought. James followed, his steps slower, heavier, as if the wet pavement were pulling at his heels.

Inside, the warmth of the house did little to ease the tension. It only made the silence feel heavier. Their home was beautiful, but tonight, it felt like a mausoleum distant, full of things they no longer touched.

Leena headed straight for the kitchen and poured herself a glass of wine. James hovered at the threshold, unsure if he should follow. The clink of the bottle against glass was loud and final.

"You coming in, or are you just going to stand there and hope I disappear again?" She said without looking at him.

He stepped inside. "I don't want to fight anymore."

Leena took a drink, leaned against the counter, and stared at him. "Then stop acting like this can be fixed with a few apologies and a quiet car ride."

He ran a hand through his hair. "I know it can't. I just... I don't know how to be in this with you anymore. Not like this."

Something in her gaze softened, but it was fleeting. "Then maybe

Just maybe we admit this is broken."

James walked to the other side of the kitchen island. He could almost touch her. Almost.

"I don't want to lose you."

"You already did," she said, her voice cracking for the first time.

The clock ticked loudly behind them. The fridge hummed. The storm outside was starting to intensify, wind pushing against the windows like something trying to get in.

James closed his eyes. "I keep thinking about the beginning. About the first time we met. That night at the bar with the broken jukebox."

Leena's lips parted. The memory flickered in her eyes.

"The song skipped halfway through," she said. "And you pretended it was fate."

He gave a faint smile. "You rolled your eyes so hard I thought you'd never look at me again."

She looked down into her wineglass. "I should've listened to my gut."

James leaned forward slightly. "I didn't mean to become this. I didn't mean for any of this to happen."

Silence fell again, but it was different now heavier and yet charged.

"Do you remember the car?" He asked suddenly.

Leena looked up, startled. "What about it?"

"That weekend we took off. No phones. No distractions. Just us. You packed three books. I brought two bottles of wine and forgot every charger."

She chuckled, despite herself. "And we lit the fire with old receipts."

"That was probably the last time we were happy," he said quietly. "Before life started to erode everything."

Leena walked past him and sat at the edge of the couch in the living room. "Life didn't erode anything, James. You stopped showing up.

James sat beside her. Outside, thunder rolled. Rain lashed against the windows.

They sat in silence, now side-by-side, not touching, but it was something.

Leena finally spoke. "You want to know the truth?"

James nodded.

"I don't know if I miss you, or just the idea of what we used to be."

James stared at the floor.

Leena set her wineglass down and stood. "I'm going to bed."

"Leena... "

She turned back. "Just stop."

She left him there, surrounded by silence and memory.

James didn't move. He just sat there, blinking slowly, trying to remember what it felt like to be forgiven.

He sat there for what might've been hours, watching the rain through the large living room windows. The fireplace, unused for months, seemed almost accusatory. He thought about lighting it. About how warmth could still live in this house if either of them remembered how to start a fire again.

He wandered to the bookshelf once their shared temple of escape and ran his hand across the spines. Travel guides from their honeymoon. Poetry Leena used to recite in the bath. A dusty copy of The Great Gatsby, with notes in the margins, her handwriting winding through it.

He pulled it down and flipped through it, searching for a moment that meant something. A passage was underlined in red ink: "I wasn't actually in love, but felt a sort of tender curiosity." Below it, Leena had written: Sounds like you.

James let out a shaky laugh. The kind that hurt more coming out than staying in.

He sat back on the couch, the book in his lap. For the first time in a long time, he wanted to say something real. Not perform. Not defend. Just admit. Just let it bleed.

But she was already upstairs.

He heard the bedroom door close upstairs. Not a slam. Just the quiet, resolute sound of someone choosing distance.

He couldn't bring himself to go upstairs. Not yet. He needed to sit with the shame, the crushing intimacy of being left just enough to feel the weight but not enough to feel release. Part of him believed that if he sat there long enough, time might just choke and spit out a different version of the night. One where they came home laughing. One where the storm was just weather.

The house creaked slightly with the wind outside. Rain hit the windows like fingers tapping glass, persistent and soft. He listened to the sound of the wind catching the corner of the porch roof, tugging it like a breath held too long.

He finally stood and walked into the kitchen, poured himself some whiskey, and leaned against the counter where Leena had stood just an hour earlier. The wine glass she'd abandoned was still there, half-full, her lipstick faintly visible on the rim. He stared at it like it might offer him an answer.

Everything in the house had become a relic. A bookmark from their anniversary trip still wedged into a coffee table book. A cracked phone charger he promised to replace. A birthday card he bought and never gave her. All of it haunted him with the ghosts of a man he used to be.

He wandered into the hallway and stared at the photographs lining the walls. He saw the timeline. Laughter in Paris, kisses in autumn leaves, their first Christmas in the house. In each one, their smiles were real. He remembered how tightly she'd held his hand back then, like she believed it was the safest place on Earth.

He grabbed his glass and wandered upstairs, his footsteps deliberately slow. He paused at the bedroom door, hand hovering, but he didn't knock.

Instead, he turned and walked into the spare room.

The sheets were stiff. The guest bed sagged slightly in the center, like even it had grown tired of waiting. He sat on the edge, stared at the wall for several minutes, then finally lay down, shoes still on. The ceiling above him was just blank silence.

His phone buzzed once on the nightstand.

He didn't move. Didn't look. He had nothing left. Emotionally stripped down, he lay motionless, burdened by the weight of what hadn't been said. Whatever that buzz was, it could wait. The world could wait. Because he couldn't carry one more thing tonight not hope, not regret.

Down the hall, Leena lay awake too. Staring at the ceiling fan. Listening to the storm. To the silence. To the past unraveling through every tick of the clock.

She wasn't sure if she wanted him to come to her or if she needed him not to.

She thought about the man who used to write her notes on napkins. Who once drove across town in the middle of the night just to leave a Polaroid on her windshield that said, "You're my favorite accident." She thought about that version of him the way someone thinks about summer in the dead of winter close, almost warm, but out of reach.

She glanced at her phone. Her thumb hovered over his name. She tapped it.

It rang once. Then again.

She hung up before voicemail could pick up. She couldn't risk hearing his voice and knowing it wasn't meant for her anymore.

She typed: "I can't sleep." Deleted it. "Come here." Deleted that too. "Please." Gone.

She set the phone down gently, as if not to wake the ghosts in the walls.

James never picked up his phone. Never checked the screen. Never saw her name.

He just lay there, staring at nothing, the light from the missed call dimming quietly beside him. In his chest, something ached he just couldn't name it anymore.

Leena curled up beneath the blanket, telling herself it didn't matter. That it was better this way. That reaching out was a moment of weakness.

They both needed the other.

They both chose silence.

He didn't sleep.

His body lay still, but his mind was a spinning reel of memory. Every sharp word. Every missed opportunity. He thought about their wedding vows how he had promised to be her anchor, her lighthouse, her storm shelter. All he had become was rust.

He stood just before dawn, the sky outside still a bruised shade of night. Moving through the house like a specter he grabbed a pen and one of the sticky pads from the junk drawer. He didn't know what he planned to write maybe a confession, maybe an apology. Maybe just her name, like that alone could mean something again.

Instead, he stood at the kitchen counter, unmoving.

Upstairs, Leena's eyes finally closed. Not sleep just surrender. Her pillow was damp on one side, but her breathing evened out in the quiet that followed. A dream almost came. A version of them laughing in the morning sun, sharing toast with a little one.

She reached for him in her sleep and touched only the cold space between them.

The sun began its slow crawl over the horizon, casting pale light through the rain-smeared windows. A new day had arrived. But nothing felt new.

Downstairs, James remained in the kitchen a lot longer than he meant to. The sticky note he'd pulled from the drawer was still blank, clutched in his hand. The pen never touched it. He couldn't find the words.

Everything felt like a lie or a half-truth or too late. He dropped it on the counter beside the mail and the list Leena had written three days ago neatly lettered, hopeful, ordinary.

He wanted to tear it all up.

He poured more of whiskey into the glass and took it with him into the living room, where he sat staring at nothing. Outside, the storm had eased into a gentle drizzle. The sky was soft, bruised, gold at the edges, like it had survived something. It pissed him off.

In the quiet, his ears picked up everything, the hum of the refrigerator, the soft whine of the heater, the creak of the house settling. Even the absence of Leena's footsteps like a missing heartbeat.

He knew her rhythms like his own. He could sense her awake upstairs, the same way he used to sense her smile from across a crowded room.

She hadn't come down.

She wouldn't.

He thought again about checking his phone. It still sat face-down on the nightstand upstairs, unbothered by the chaos it carried. Part of him knew it wouldn't just be a notification. It would be something fragile, her name, her voice, a thread he'd be too afraid to pull.

Instead, he leaned his head back against the couch, closed his eyes, and let the guilt soak in.

Upstairs, Leena stirred but didn't get up. Her hand hovered above her phone again, even now. Just one message, she thought. One line. It wouldn't fix anything, but maybe it could stop the unraveling.

She typed out: "Still awake."

She stared at it. Erased it. Tried again: "Do you want coffee?"

She erased that too.

Then finally: "I miss you."

And deleted it.

The house remained quiet. The message unsent. The silence intact.

She eventually drifted into a dreamless, weighted sleep, her breath shallow and uneven. The pillow held her warmth, but her body felt cold, the kind of cold that seeps into your bones when you've spent too long waiting on something or someone that never comes.

James still hadn't moved from the couch.

The whiskey in his glass was long gone, nothing but drops clinging to the bottom. He turned the empty glass in his hands like it held some truth. His mind kept replaying the night on an endless loop her voice, the rain, the sharpness in her eyes when she looked at him like that was the end.

He finally stood and walked over to the fireplace, where an old box of photos sat.

He hadn't touched it in years. Inside were Polaroids, ticket stubs, notes she'd left him over the years. A napkin from their first date. Her doodles from when she got bored during long drives. Things that seemed too small to hold onto at the time, and now felt too sacred to throw away.

He sifted through them, his fingers trembling. There was one photo he lingered on a blurry candid of her, laughing, hand over her mouth, caught mid-snort in a booth of a restaurant. She hated that picture. He loved it because she wasn't performing for anyone. She wasn't guarded. She was just... Leena.

He wanted to crawl into that photo. He wanted to hand it to the man he used to be and say, "Don't screw this up. She's already perfect."
He set it on the mantel. Just to see her face somewhere besides in his regrets.

Upstairs, Leena stirred again. Not because of a noise but because something inside her cracked wide open. A memory, maybe. Or the echo of love that wouldn't quite die no matter how many times she stabbed it with disappointment. She sat up and stared at the door like it might open.

It didn't.

The sun began to bleed into the room, touching everything softly, like even it knew not to be too loud. Her eyes stung from little sleep and too much pretending.

Downstairs, James stood in front of the fireplace, the photo still in view. He took a step back, shoulders slumped.

Maybe, he thought, today would bring answers. Or at the very least the courage to stop running from the questions.

He took the old photo with him to the couch and sat, staring at it like it was proof that magic had once lived between them. He wanted to speak to it. But he sat with the ache in his chest and the silence that filled the house like fog.

The clock on the wall ticked louder than it had any right to. Each second scraped past like a reminder: you could have gone to her.

You could have acted like a decent human when she was curled up on the bathroom floor. He didn't. He hadn't. And now, every tick was a verdict.

In her room, Leena blinked back tears she couldn't explain. Her body was exhausted. She buried her face in the pillow and whispered a name that didn't answer back.

She wasn't crying over the fight. She was mourning the slow death of the relationship.

And James, only feet away, sat in the dim light thinking the same thing.

They weren't just two people with unresolved issues. They were once the fire. Now, just smoke curling up from things neither had the tools to rebuild or the nerve to bury.

He leaned forward, elbows on his knees, rubbing his hands together like he could start something, but the only thing that came was another sigh. He looked over at the mantle again, that photo of her.

He whispered to it, finally.

"I'm still in here, you know."

It wasn't loud. It wasn't brave. But it was honest.

Upstairs, Leena hadn't moved, but her body had stopped resisting sleep. She sank into it slowly, as if the silence were a current pulling her under. The lump in her throat didn't go away, but it softened, dulled by exhaustion and the quiet admission that tonight, they both had lost.

James stretched out across the couch, letting his legs dangle off the edge like he used to on lazy Sundays. But there was no music playing. No sunlight streaming through the curtains. Just the dim, grey light of early morning and the soft hum of everything.

He closed his eyes.

But for a moment, he stopped thinking.

He let the morning stretch around him in silence. The light crawling up the walls like it didn't want to intrude. Still holding the photo, James rested it on his chest as he lay back again.

Not asleep. Not awake. Somewhere in the middle only grief can manufacture.

He thought of a hundred things he should've said. Should've done. Thought about the old argument they'd never really had the one where she finally admitted she'd been holding on too tightly.

In the room above, Leena stirred again. She sat up, hugged her knees to her chest, and watched the sunlight crawl over the windowpane. It painted thin lines on the floor, gold slicing through grey. Her phone sat inches away, quiet.

She whispered aloud, "You still there?"

She didn't mean for him to hear it. She didn't expect an answer.

But James, down below, exhaled. Almost at the same time.

They didn't know it yet, but something was still tethered. Fragile. Razor thin. But real.

The house breathed with it.

James eventually rose from the couch, not because he felt better, but because the weight of stillness had grown unbearable.

In another life, he would've walked upstairs. Climbed into bed. Apologized with the kind of truth that bleeds. But he was still that version of himself that flinched from vulnerability and called it strength. So instead, he stood there and watched the sky brighten.

Leena, though, her sleep was restless. Her dreams were a haze of voices: his, hers, and ones she didn't recognize. None of them said what needed saying.

The air held like breath caught between two lips.

He stood for a long moment, staring into the dim glow of the kitchen. Then, almost without thinking, he reached for the sticky note again. This time, the pen touched paper.

The words didn't come all at once. They arrived cautiously, like he was afraid the page might reject the ink.

"What if we just left for a while? A cabin. By the lake. No phones. No noise. Just breathing. We used to be good at breathing."

He stared at it, chewed the cap of the pen, then added one more line: "If you want to go, let me know. Or just pack a bag. I'll drive."

He folded the note in half, then thought better of it. Unfolded it. Left it just the way it was raw, open, unsure.

He placed it beneath the base of her wine glass on the counter, careful not to smear her lipstick mark on the rim. A piece of him wanted her to see both at once the note and the ghost of where her mouth had been. Proof that she was still here. That he still noticed.

Only then did he finally climb the stairs again, moving slowly, each step a mile.

He didn't pause at their bedroom this time.

He walked into the spare room, pulled off his shoes without un-tying them, and collapsed into the stiff bed. The sheets smelled like dust and old air. But for the first time in hours, he let himself breathe.

It wasn't peace.

But it was something close.

Chapter 3

Later in the day, the light crept in slowly, dragging itself across the room, colorless light across the house. Leena blinked softly waking up slowly, the weight of the night still sitting on her chest like a dream she hadn't pulled her self out of yet. Her eyes found the ceiling first, then her phone, then the faint imprint on the pillow where James used to sleep.

She didn't reach for the phone. She didn't call out. She didn't expect him to be there anymore. But when she finally pushed herself awake, and walked into the hall, her eyes caught a glint of glass on the kitchen counter below.

Curious, cautious, she walked down the stairs. The house was silent, save for the faint drip of rainwater sliding off the gutters. Her fingers brushed along the edge of the stair rail, grounding herself in as she moved toward whatever came next.

The wine glass was still sitting where she had left it. But underneath it she saw it.

A note.

Folded carefully. The ink smudged at the edge.

"What if we just left for a while? A cabin. By the lake. No phones. No noise. Just breathing. We used to be good at breathing.

If you want to go, let me know. Or just pack a bag. I'll drive."

Her fingers slightly touching it before picking it up. She read it twice. Then a third time.

She didn't cry. Not yet. But the metaphorical wall she'd been leaning on shifted slightly, like it was considering falling.

Upstairs, James was awake but didn't move. The guest bed was uncomfortable, but the silence was worse. He stared at the ceiling, half-daring himself to hope. He didn't know if she'd find the note. He had no idea if she'd even read it, didn't know if she'd feel anything at all if she did.

Downstairs, she was noticing the wine glass, untouched since the night before. She picked it up, the stale scent making her feel slightly sick. After a pause, she set it back down.

Drinking was not happening today. Not after the night they'd just endured. Instead, she held the note in both hands, gripping it like it might dissolve if she let go, letting the weight of the afternoon sunlight settle around her.

And for the first time in days, her shoulders slumped. Just a little.

She glanced up the stairs.

Then she walked to the cabinet, grabbed her sketchbook and a charcoal pencil, and opened a clean page.

She just sat with the pencil hovering over the page, letting her thoughts spill out on the counter-top that she wasn't sure how to tie together. Her mind wasn't empty, it was loud. Echoing with last night's fight and the way James had looked at her... like he didn't recognize her anymore. Maybe, she thought, she didn't recognize herself.

Minutes passed.

She finally sketched a line. Then another. Slow, deliberate strokes that weren't meant to be beautiful. They were just honest. A lake, maybe. Some trees. A suggestion of stillness. She didn't try to erase smudges. Didn't care if the lines were jagged.

She heard the floor shift upstairs and paused, listening. But no footsteps followed. Just a quiet shuffling of someone still deciding whether to face the day or avoid it.

She looked back at the note, rereading the words that felt like they'd been pulled from somewhere deeper than apology. Not so much a promise. But maybe an opening.

Leena stood, walked to the back door, and opened it just enough to feel the outside air. It was cool and damp with a hint of rain. The sky was still overcast.

She breathed it in. She whispered, "Maybe."

Upstairs, James rolled onto his side, staring at the wall. His heart beat a little harder. He didn't know why.

She lingered there at the backdoor, hand resting on the knob like it was a decision she hadn't made yet. The air smelled like damp leaves and soil, like the start of something new. Something possible.

Back at the table, her sketch had begun to take shape. Not a cabin exactly but the essence of it. Quiet. Empty yet inviting. A winding path led to the lake where a rowboat sat tied to a dock. In the distance, she'd drawn two chairs on a porch. No people. Just space.

She set down the pencil and stared at what she sketched for a long time. The kind of staring that wasn't about seeing, just absorbing.

She could almost feel the way the air might taste out there: pine, woodsmoke, and the faint trace of rain in the wind. She imagined the silence. It was the good kind of silence. The kind you didn't need to fill with anything at all.

For the first time in a long time, she didn't feel like running.

Leena folded the note once more and slipped it into the sketchbook between the pages. A keepsake.

The creak of the stairs upstairs told her James had moved. Just a little. The silence shifted again. Like a held breath that hadn't quite been released.

She glanced back at the wine glass and thought quietly: Maybe I'll pack a bag.

She turned toward the hallway and disappeared back into the house.

Upstairs, James on his back in the guest bed, eyes open, watching shadows stretch across the ceiling like veins under skin. He hadn't really slept. just drifted in and out of anxious half-consciousness, caught between the silence and the hope that something might have changed.

He kept imagining what she looked like when she read the note. Did she care? Did she roll her eyes? Cry? Did she crumple it? Did she just toss it away? He didn't know. He didn't even know if he wanted to be forgiven. He knew he didn't deserve it. He needed her to know that he was still trying, though. That the part of him that remembered how to love her wasn't dead, it was just buried under layers of pride.

He remembered when Leena had tried to repaint the hallway herself, insisting they didn't need to hire someone. She'd spilled the white paint all over her black leggings and cursed so colorfully that he'd laughed until his stomach hurt. She'd thrown a sponge at him. Then kissed him.

That memory made his throat tighten.

He wondered what she was doing now. If she'd gone outside. If she was already packing. Or if she was upstairs again, wondering if it was too late.

James exhaled and sat up slowly. His body ached in the way that only guilt can settle into joints. But somewhere beneath the ache, there was a pulse of something else: anticipation. Not hope, not yet.

He stood and walked quietly to the bedroom door, pressing his hand against it as if feeling the temperature of the house through wood.
Maybe today wasn't about fixing everything. Maybe it was just about opening the door.

He didn't open the door. Not just physically or even emotionally. More in his head. Like standing up for the first time after being buried.

He thought about leaving, like a reset button. A quiet place someone else had built for fun or maybe even living, tucked away by a lake, waiting for new stories to be written in its stillness. He pictured Leena there, not saying much, just standing in the light that slanted through the pines, holding a mug of coffee in both hands. Paint-smeared fingers, her hair down, that soft wrinkle between her brows when she got lost in her mind. She had been most alive in stillness.

He remembered the first time she brought him to a place like that. It was not long after they'd started dating. A borrowed weekend in an Airbnb with spotty cell reception and chipped teacups. She'd dragged him out to the dock before sunrise, laughing at how grumpy he was, wrapped in blankets. She'd painted the trees while he dozed beside her, then kissed him like the silence had wound her heart tighter to his.

James shut his eyes, breathed in the memory. A longing for what had once felt effortless. They'd lost that ease somewhere between resentment.

But maybe if he could hold space again instead of control, if he could show her instead of convince her maybe there was still something to salvage. Something to rebuild with open hands.

He glanced toward the guest room window. The light had changed again. Warmer. Like the house itself was leaning forward to listen.

He stepped away from the door, moving instead to the window, pulling the curtain aside with two fingers. Outside, the light had softened to a dim, introspective hue.

He stood there, watching the trees sway in the wind, wondering what Leena was feeling right now. Whether she was angry, or sad, or something more complicated. Maybe something beyond language. He thought about the note. Whether it had landed the way he meant it to or whether it had just stirred the waters more.

He leaned his head against the cool glass, eyes following the outline of a single leaf tumbling in the breeze. Everything felt weightless and heavy at the same time.

He didn't reach for his suitcase. Not yet. Not while the air between them was still thick with uncertainty and unspoken things. For now, he stayed there at the window, not moving, just hoping the next sound he heard would be her voice.

Memories of the night before crept in. How her voice had cracked when she shouted, how he'd looked away when she needed him to meet her gaze, and how she'd stormed up the stairs yet he didn't follow. There was always something left unsaid.

He rubbed his hands together, a nervous habit, then pressed them to his face. The silence in the house wasn't empty.

It felt like standing in the eye of a storm that had already passed but it was way too dark to see what damage was left in its wake.

He wanted to move. To act. But every instinct told him to wait. To let her decide if she would answer. He had sent the invitation and he knew that was all he could offer without turning it into something else

He wondered if she was still downstairs, sitting with the note, or if she'd tucked it away

Maybe she was painting again. Maybe she was crying. Maybe she was just sitting in the doorway like she had earlier, letting the cool air touch her skin and pretending it could reach her heart.

A floorboard creaked somewhere in the house and his head lifted listening.

But it passed. Just the skeleton of the house settling, not Leena.

So James sat there, caught in the gravity of all he hadn't said, waiting for something: small a footstep, a breath, a whisper that might mean she was still with him, in some way. Waiting for anything.

The weight of stillness was starting to fray his nerves. James leaned back against the headboard and closed his eyes, trying to silence the loops in his mind. But they kept saying the words he could've said, the look in her eyes when he didn't.

He had hurt her in ways she hadn't even noticed yet, and maybe she wouldn't. Maybe she was beyond talking now. But something about the way she looked at him in the hallway last night, like she was seeing someone else wearing his skin, had stayed lodged in his head.

He shifted again, staring up at the ceiling, tracing the pattern of specks in the plaster. They reminded him of stars they used to watch together. Laying on their backs in the bed of his truck, parked out in the middle of nowhere in the country. She would point and invent names for ones that didn't exist, and he would nod like he was learning something.

He missed that version of her. The one that still let herself believe in little myths. The one who looked at the sky like it would have a conversation with her.

And he missed the version of himself that had earned her gaze.

A gust of wind rattled a loose shutter somewhere outside. James sat up again, ran his hands through his hair, and stared at the door across the room...imagining her on the other side of it.

He wished he could say something, anything. But he knew that if he spoke too soon, too carelessly, it could undo everything. So instead, he whispered into the quiet of the room:

"Don't screw this up. You can't. Not again."

He stood, walked back to the window, and placed his palm flat against the glass like he was reaching through it. In the distance, the trees moved like they were exhaling. Somewhere below, the faintest creak of a cabinet door echoed up through the vents.

He closed his eyes.

She was still moving. Still there.

Downstairs, Leena's phone vibrated against the kitchen counter. She nearly ignored it, assuming it was some notification she didn't have the energy for.

But something about the name that flashed on the screen made her pick it up. It was Sofia.

She answered on the third ring, voice still low with sleep and unrest. "Hey."

"Leen," Sofia said softly. "I just wanted to check on you. You okay?"

Leena exhaled through her nose, sliding a hand through her hair, not knowing James had just done the same. "Not really. But… maybe. I don't know."

"You sounded horrible before you left. I didn't want to pry."

"It was bad," Leena admitted. "He left me a note."

James, upstairs, paused. He hadn't meant to listen, but the vent channeled just enough of her voice through the floorboards where he could hear her speaking.

"A note?" Sofia said. "What do you mean a note?"

"He said we should get away. Somewhere quiet. Just breathe. He didn't push. Just… left it on the counter for me to find."

There was a long pause, and then Sofia asked gently, "well?"

Leena didn't answer right away. But James heard it: the breath she took before replying.

"Yeah," she said finally. "I guess so."

James let his eyes close. Just for a second. The tension in his shoulders didn't disappear but it eased.

Downstairs, Leena ended the call and leaned against the counter, phone still in hand. She didn't need to tell James, but she wanted him to know she'd heard him.

For the first time in a long while, she felt like going somewhere.

Leena sat at the counter after the call ended, the cool mug grounding her as her mind spun. She didn't even remember pouring the coffee, but there it was, half full and untouched.

She walked back to the sketchbook and reopened it. Her fingers hovered over the rough charcoal lines of the drawing she'd started: soft trees, muted sky, the slope of a roof line. Her thumb smudged a shadow into something more organic.

In the stillness, her eyes wandered the room. Noting his absence like a bruise she'd forgotten until she pressed it.

A half-folded blanket on the couch. His hoodie slung over a kitchen chair. It all felt temporary. Like neither of them had unpacked in days, even if they'd never technically left.

As she took a sip of the now-lukewarm coffee. With her free hand, she picked up the note again.

She didn't read it this time. She just held it.
Then, as if the quiet had opened a door, she said aloud, "Okay."

Upstairs, James had been holding his breath. The sound of her voice muffled by the walls but clear in intent washed over him like warm rain.

He didn't smile. The tension in his chest cracked.

Leena stayed where she was, her hand still resting on the kitchen counter, her thoughts as scattered as the morning light that now spilled through the window in golden streaks. The call from Sofia had grounded her, sure but it had also stirred something else. Something unsteady and still waking up inside her.

She hadn't expected to say yes. Not out loud. Not even to her closest friend. But the word had rolled off her tongue, now it was real.

She moved to the sink and rinsed out the coffee mug, the sound of water beneath the clinking of ceramic. Every movement felt like her body was trying to make decisions before her mind caught up.

The old house seemed to hum around her, the silence no longer suffocating.

She walked through the living room then she paused near the stairs and looked up, as if she could see through the ceiling and find him sitting on the edge of the bed. And for a moment, she wanted to call to make sure he heard her.

But instead, she whispered something quieter to herself: "I'm still here."

She turned back to the table, picked up the sketch again, and added a single figure to the page sitting in one of the chairs facing the lake.

Leena stared at the drawing for a long moment before setting the sketchbook aside and wiping her hands on her jeans. She rose from the table slowly, heart beating loud enough she could feel it in her throat.

Without letting herself think too long, she moved toward the stairs.

Her feet were soft against the wooden steps, each one creaking just enough to betray her presence. At the top, she paused. James' door was shut. It wasn't their door anymore, it was his door. She hesitated, then lifted her hand.

She knocked twice, not forceful, but soft and easy.

Inside, James stiffened. His breath caught as he turned toward the sound. His body moved before his mind, crossing the room in four quiet steps. He opened the door slowly.

Leena stood there, arms crossed. Not in anger, but more like it was in self-preservation. Her eyes flicked up to meet his. Her voice was steady, even if her chest betrayed the flutter underneath.

"I just wanted to say I'm sorry," she said. "For last night. For the way I let it get to that point."

James's throat tightened. He took a slow breath, then stepped aside.

"You don't need to apologize," he said softly. "I was just as much of the problem."

Leena didn't move to come in. Instead, her eyes softened just enough to let something human through.

He rubbed the back of his neck, his voice low. "I'm sorry too. For the way I acted. For all the nights I didn't show up when you needed me to."

She looked at him for a long time. Then, cautiously, she stepped forward. He didn't pull her in but he didn't move away either.

When her head finally rested against his chest, his arms wrapped around her slowly, like she was made of something breakable. The hug wasn't rushed. It wasn't for forgiveness. It was just to feel that they were still there. Still together.

She didn't cry. They just stood there, holding the version of each other they could still reach.

After a while, she leaned back slightly and looked up at him.

"I'm going to go pack," she said.

He nodded.

Chapter 4

And without another word, she turned and disappeared back down the hall, leaving him in the doorway. He was quiet, wrecked, and more hopeful than he had been in months.

Leena stood in front of the closet, staring at it like it might bite her. It was ridiculous how something so mundane [zippers, fabric, empty hangers] could feel like a battlefield. She had packed for dozens of trips in her life, most of them spontaneous, but this one felt like preparing to cross a line she wasn't sure either of them could uncross.

The suitcase lay behind her, its mouth yawning for decisions she hadn't yet made. She pulled a sweater from the hanger, something soft and oversized, and held it to her chest. Not because she needed warmth, but because it still smelled like cedar and campfires. Smelled like something they'd shared before the cold years crept in. She folded it, not neatly, but with care, and placed it into the suitcase.

She added jeans next, then hesitated before choosing a second pair. Why was this so hard? They weren't going off-grid for years.

Her eyes landed on a drawer she hadn't opened in months. She walked to it slowly, pulling it out with a soft creak. Inside was a scarf James had given her two winters ago. Wool, gray-blue like the sky right before snow. She held it for a moment, fingers grazing the fabric, before setting it in the suitcase too.

She paused and sat on the bed for a moment, staring at the half-filled suitcase like it might talk to her. Her mind drifted to all the conversations they'd never had, things they'd both swallowed to avoid another fight. A little voice in her head asked, "What if it's worse when we're alone? What if there's nothing left to say?" But she shook it off and pushed it away. She was done living in the questions she didn't have the answers to.

Downstairs, the soft hum of the refrigerator and the distant sound of a car passing by became the house's only soundtrack. The space between them was still thick.

James still hadn't packed. Not a bag. Not a toothbrush. It wasn't laziness, it was reverence. He didn't want to assume anything, didn't want to jinx the thread that had been stretched taut between them. Still, the nod she'd given him, quiet but real, still felt like a green light in a fog.

He peeled himself away from the hallway wall and returned to his room. The space was dim and too neat, like it had been cleaned but not lived in. He pulled an old duffel bag from the closet and tossed it on the bed, then stood there for a second, staring at it like it might be a trick.

He moved with a kind of clumsy purpose grabbing clothes from drawers, not worrying if they matched. A flannel. A hoodie. A pair of jeans that still held the scent of firewood from some forgotten fall evening. He added socks, boxers, a shaving kit he hadn't used in weeks. Every item he packed felt like a conversation.

In the back of the closet, he found the faded black beanie she used to steal on cold mornings. Without thinking, he tucked it between two shirts.

When he zipped the bag closed, it made a quiet, final sound.

He sat on the edge of the bed for a moment, elbows on his knees, palms pressed together like he was praying to the floorboards. They hadn't really spoken. Not about the trip. Not about what came after.

But somehow, it felt like the most honest exchange they'd had in months.

Leena moved methodically. Sweater. Jeans. Sketchbook. Brushes. A few tubes of paint she didn't even check, just grabbed them like a memory. She paused at a photo on the shelf near the bookshelf: it was of them, three years ago, barefoot on the lake dock, both sunburned and laughing. She didn't cry. She didn't smile. She just looked.

She didn't need to bring reminders of what they were. The point was to see if they could still become something else.

On the kitchen counter sat a thermos, dusty from disuse. She rinsed it, dried it, and filled it

She caught her reflection in the kitchen window. She looked drawn, tired, but not broken. She brushed a strand of hair from her face, whispering to herself, "Okay. One step."

James finally stepped into the hallway, stopping at the top of the stairs. He leaned against the wall, arms crossed, listening to her move around below like she was rearranging gravity.

He noticed the light change through the windows. It had gone from flat gray to something almost golden, like even the sky was trying to encourage a softer ending.

She looked up once, saw him there through the banister, and neither of them smiled. But she nodded. A small, solid nod that said, I see you.

He nodded back.

It was a fragile truce, but a truce nonetheless.

Leena moved to the hall closet and took down her coat. She paused, hand still gripping the fabric. There was a nervous flutter in her chest. Not fear, exactly. Just the awareness of change. The suitcase by the door felt like a symbol more than luggage like she was choosing to carry something besides resentment.

She found a note pad on the counter and scribbled a quick list: toothbrush, charger, socks. She folded it and stuck it in her jacket pocket. The act of writing it made her feel momentarily in control, like she had agency in a world that had felt dictated by emotional tides.

She zipped the suitcase with a final, decisive pull, then walked it to the door. James met her there a few minutes later, hoodie over one shoulder, keys in hand.

They stood there for a beat, the door closed behind them. Not quite together. Not quite apart.

"I'll drive," he said.

"I read that," she replied, her voice low but not cold.
She stepped through the door first. He followed.

The sun had finally broken through the clouds. The light fell across the porch and caught the edge of her hair, turning it almost gold. James glanced at it. Noticing it but not grabbing it.

She glanced over her shoulder. "You sure you're ready for this?"

He exhaled through his nose, almost a laugh. "I'm not sure of anything. But I want to try."

Leena didn't say anything. But she nodded again. This one softer. Maybe even forgiving.

They walked to the car slowly, side by side but still carrying separate silences. She placed her suitcase in the trunk herself, then slid into the passenger seat. James opened his door, stood for a beat longer, then got in. He didn't start the engine right away. They just sat there, letting it settle.

And when he finally turned the key, it wasn't with certainty but with hope.

Chapter 5

The drive started in silence. Not heavy, not uncomfortable just quiet. The kind that lets the road hum beneath you, where the trees blur into watercolor streaks and time stops tapping its foot for a while.

James kept his hands at ten and two, eyes on the road, jaw tight. Not clenched. Just held. Leena sat with her elbow on the armrest, her fingers idly curled under her chin, watching the trees slip by like she was waiting for the forest to say something.

No music, He didn't turn any on. No podcasts. No filler. Just them and the low purr of the engine and the occasional whir of passing cars.

The sky above them was a canvas of pale gray, the kind that looked like it might rain or clear at any moment, but refused to commit. The further they drove, the more the city fell away behind them. The strip malls, gas stations, and traffic lights thinning out until even the roads started to feel unfamiliar.

A few miles in, James glanced over. She hadn't moved. But her phone was in her hand now, screen glowing as her thumb tapped deliberately. She was searching.

He didn't ask what for.

She didn't look up.

A few more miles passed before she said softly, "Do you think a lake house is too predictable?"

He blinked. "What?"

She tapped a few more times. "There's this place pretty secluded. Middle of nowhere. Real fireplace. No TV."

James lifted his chin slightly, eyes still forward. "Sounds like the kind of place people go to either make up or murder each other."

Leena almost smiled. Almost. "I'm not ruling either out."

A breath of shared humor passed between them.

She clicked the link, scanned the listing. It had everything they didn't know they needed. Solitude. Stillness. Enough space between the walls to not speak if they didn't want to. Rustic charm without pretense. A claw-foot tub. A view of the lake that stretching out like a secret.

"I booked it," she said a few minutes later.

James nodded. Not a casual nod but a real one. Like something had just been agreed to silently.

The road curved, and he adjusted the wheel without thinking. Leena leaned her head against the window, her breath fogging a small patch of glass. She drew a lazy spiral into it with her finger.

He nodded slowly. "You used to draw them everywhere. Napkins. Receipts. The back of my hand."

A faint smile touched her lips. "You never minded."

"I liked watching you draw them. It meant you were still... Somewhere else. But safe."

She let the words settle, didn't comment on them. Just pressed her forehead to the glass and closed her eyes for a few seconds.

Out the window, the landscape began to shift. The trees grew taller, older. The houses became scarcer, then disappeared altogether. James turned down a narrow road lined with towering pines, the car's tires crunching faintly over gravel.

He didn't know if they were ready. If anything they were doing made sense. But in that moment, he was just grateful the silence wasn't suffocating.

"I'll send them the check-in info when we get closer," Leena said, voice soft. "It's a key code on the door. No hosts. No neighbors."

"No witnesses?" He teased, trying to keep the joke alive.

Leena gave a soft laugh. "Just deer and ghosts."

James smiled, barely. But it stayed.

They drove on, further from everything they knew and toward something they didn't.

The road narrowed even more, as if the world itself were funneling them into a quieter place, almost like time folded away from everything else. Trees pressed in closer on either side, their bare branches arching overhead like cathedral beams, and for a brief moment of time, neither of them spoke.

James adjusted the rear view mirror. His grip loosened on the steering wheel. Something about the way the road curved ahead made him feel like this stretch, this unknown, had a pulse of its own.

Leena scrolled through her phone, though the booking was already confirmed. The image of the cottage was still open on her screen. A weathered wood exterior, the lake barely visible in the distance behind it. It looked like a place forgotten by time, like it had survived simply because no one had asked anything of it.

"Two bedrooms," she said, barely above a whisper.

James glanced over. "I figured."

Another stretch of silence.

"I didn't want to assume," she added.

"You didn't," he replied. But the words felt like gravel in his throat.

They passed a roadside fruit stand boarded up for the season. A few crows lingered on the sign, pecking at nothing. James caught himself wondering how many couples had driven this same road for the same reasons needing space, needing quiet, needing something that didn't exist back home.

A few more turns and they came upon a clearing. The lake glittered distantly through the trees, dark and still, like it was holding its breath for them. The wind pushed softly against the car, nudging them forward.

Leena finally looked over at James. "It feels like we're driving into a story."

He nodded. "Hopefully not a tragedy."

"No," she said. "I think we've already read through that part."

James let that settle for a moment, the weight of her words pressing lightly against his chest like a hand. Not dramatic. Just real. Honest in a way that neither of them had allowed themselves to be in far too long.

The tires crunched over loose gravel, echoing softly through the trees. They passed a weathered wooden sign half-swallowed by moss that read "Lake Darrow – 3 Miles." Neither of them had heard of it before last night. That felt right.

Leena pulled her legs up into the seat, wrapping her arms around her knees as she turned her body slightly toward him. "You remember that trip we took to Crescent Hollow?"

James nodded, eyes still forward. "You mean the one where you got food poisoning from gas station sushi?"

A soft laugh slipped from her throat. "Yeah. That one."

"How could I forget? You threw up in a vase."

"It was decorative! I was desperate."

"You apologized to it."

This time, the laugh bloomed fuller. Genuine. She leaned her head against the seat, her eyes closing as if the sound of her own laughter startled her.

"That trip was a mess," she said softly.

James glanced at her. "Still one of my favorites."

Her eyes opened, hazel catching the soft glow outside. "Why?"

He hesitated, as if sifting through the pieces. "Because we weren't trying to be anything. We just were. Even in the middle of everything falling apart."

She looked down at her hands. Her fingers twisted the hem of her sleeve, her voice barely audible. "I miss that."

James slowed the car a little as they approached a curve, and for a long moment, the only sound was the rhythm of the road beneath them.

Ahead, a deer darted across the lane, vanishing just as quickly into the brush. James hit the brakes, not hard, just enough. Their bodies rocked forward and back in unison.

They both looked at the place where the deer had disappeared, their breaths synchronized. James drove on.

"I'm not saying this will be a fix," James murmured.

Leena didn't look away from the trees. "I know. But it might stop the bleeding."

They sat with that.

The road continued to unfold in front of them, like a story still being written.

A small town gave way to trees once more, and as the road unspooled in front of them, James glanced at her briefly. Her profile against the amber light looked softer now. Tired, yes, but untangled and less guarded.

James slowed as they approached the turnoff for the cabin. "You think we'll be able to sleep tonight?"

Leena didn't answer right away. She was watching the lake reappear between the trees. "Maybe not great. But maybe better."

The gravel crunched under them again as they pulled into the clearing. The cabin stood waiting, windows catching the gold of sunset. Not watching exactly, but just there. Like it had always been.

It was rustic but charming, like something out of a old book. Weathered cedar planks formed the exterior, softened by moss at the base and patches of ivy that crept up the western wall. A narrow porch wrapped around one side, complete with a crooked rocking chair and a chipped enamel mug resting on the railing, as if someone had only just left. The front door, painted a deep hunter green, looked worn but solid.

Surrounding the cabin, the woods exhaled the scent of pine and damp earth. Trees stood tall and quiet like sentinels, their branches swaying gently as the breeze wandered between them. The lake behind the cabin shimmered in the lowering sun, still and glassy, cradled in a hush that felt older than time. A pair of loons called somewhere in the distance, haunting and sweet, echoing across the water.

The air felt cleaner here: crisp, cool, with the faintest trace of smoke from a distant fireplace or an old chimney that hadn't quite let go of its last ember. It clung to their skin.

Inside, the cabin surprised them. It had modern amenities. A small but functional kitchen with a gas stove, a stainless steel sink, and even a French press resting beside a bag of locally roasted coffee. There was electricity, hot water, and even flushing toilets, which Leena half-jokingly praised like they were a five-star feature.

The living room was dimly lit with warm yellow sconces and a single bulb pendant hanging over a battered coffee table. A crackling stone fireplace dominated one wall, flanked by bookshelves bursting with dog-eared novels, mismatched poetry collections, and a few faded maps of hiking trails long grown over.

In the corner sat an old record player, still functional, its speakers humming faintly with static when James flicked it on. A stack of vinyls leaned beside it including Coltrane, Joni Mitchell, Patsy Cline, a few jazz albums whose covers had yellowed with time. Next to the fireplace stood a bar cart stocked like someone had planned to weather a storm: bourbon, scotch, wine, and enough mixers to entertain a dozen guests who'd never arrive.

Leena trailed her fingers over the bar's polished wood, then turned slowly in a full circle, taking it all in. "It's perfect," she whispered.

James didn't say anything, but the way his shoulders finally dropped said enough.

They walked slowly through the rest of the cabin, exploring the bedrooms, each of them modest but cozy, with thick quilts folded neatly at the foot of the beds and windows that opened to nothing but trees and distant water. The walls were paneled in warm pine, and the floors creaked softly underfoot, like the house had its own sleepy breath.

In the smaller bedroom, a hand-painted sign hung above the bed: Rest easy. It made Leena pause. She didn't say anything about it. Just stared for a few heartbeats longer than necessary.

Back in the main room, a worn leather armchair sat beside the fireplace, its arms smooth from use. A basket of firewood rested nearby, and beside it, an old wool blanket was folded atop a trunk that doubled as a coffee table. James knelt to open the trunk. Inside were old board games like Scrabble, checkers, a faded deck of cards and a guest book filled with notes from visitors who had come before. Some of the messages were cryptic, even poetic. Others were simple, like "We came here to fall in love. We did."

Outside, a small path led from the porch to a dock that jutted out over the lake. They followed it quietly, their boots crunching on the worn wooden boards. The lake stretched before them, still asleep. Reflections of treetops swirled in the glassy water, broken only by the occasional ripple of a fish near the surface.

A cool breeze danced over the water, carrying the scent of pine needles, moss, and something faintly metallic like old rain and secrets.

Leena closed her eyes and inhaled deeply, her chest rising slowly, as if trying to fill herself with all of it.

James leaned against the railing of the dock, watching the sky bleed from amber to deep lavender. "This place... It feels like it was made to be forgotten."

Leena opened her eyes. "Or remembered."

They stood there for a while longer, letting the silence between them stretch and settle. When they finally turned back toward the cabin, it wasn't with urgency, but with a shared sense of purpose. Not resolution, but something in the area of it.

Once inside again, Leena wandered into the bathroom and paused.

"James?" She called out, the disbelief in her voice.

"Yeah?"

"There's not a single roll of toilet paper in this place."

James chuckled, appearing in the doorway. "What, you don't want to go full survival and use leaves?"

Leena gave him a flat look. "I swear to God, if I come back with a rash, you're sleeping in the woods."

He raised both hands in mock surrender. "Okay, okay. TP goes at the top of the list."

They gathered at the small kitchen table, pulling open drawers until they found a pen and a notepad that looked like it belonged in a motel lobby. Leena flipped to a blank page and scribbled across the top: Emergency Supplies.

"Toilet paper," she said aloud, writing it in all caps.

"Food," James added. "Something real. Not just wine and crackers."

"Pancake stuff," Leena chimed in. "Flour, eggs, milk, syrup…"

"Bacon. Can't have pancakes without bacon."

"Fruit."

"Coffee filters. I don't trust that French press to get us through the week."

They kept adding to the list vegetables, snacks, batteries, a flashlight, extra blankets just in case. The GPS had already proven spotty, so James grabbed the folded-up paper map they'd found in the trunk and spread it out on the table.

"There's a town and it looks like it's not that far," he said, pointing. "Might have a grocery store. Or at least somewhere that doesn't just sell bait and beer."

Leena leaned over his shoulder, her hair brushing his cheek without either of them pulling away. "Let's hope so. I'm not in the mood to MacGyver anything."

James grinned. "If we have to we could always raid a gas station for toilet paper but I think I'm too civilized for single ply."

She laughed genuinely, freely and folded the list in half.

"Let's go scavenge," she said.

And just like that, they stepped back into the world, side by side, searching for the pieces to hold them together again even if it started with something as simple as toilet paper.

They didn't go straight to the store. They spotted a weathered roadside sign that read "Millie's Diner: Home of the Best Pie in the Pines. "Next left." It pointed down a short gravel lane tucked behind a grove of birch trees.

James turned without asking. Leena didn't protest.

The diner was a time capsule of chrome trim, checkerboard floors, red vinyl booths, and neon signs that buzzed faintly overhead. The scent of frying bacon and fresh coffee met them at the door, along with the gentle chime of a bell. Behind the counter, a woman with gray curls and a pencil tucked behind her ear waved at them like they were expected.

They chose a booth by the window. A table top jukebox in the corner crooned out a soft, static-laced version of "It's Been a Long, Long Time." Leena closed her eyes for a second, recognizing the tune.

James smirked, gesturing toward the speaker. "Endgame, last scene. I teared up like a punk in the theater."

Leena raised an eyebrow. "I remember....I thought we were going to have to leave."

"I'm a man of depth and dignity. Shut up."

She laughed under her breath. "You're such a nerd."

"You married me anyway."

"Questionable."

The server came by with two menus and a tired but kind smile. They ordered without overthinking coffee, pancakes, eggs, toast, and a slice of peach pie because it felt criminal not to.

While they waited, Leena pulled out her phone. A single bar of signal flickered in the corner of the screen.

She typed out a message to Sofia:

"Made it. Staying in a cabin near Lake Darrow. No service. Just in case."

She hovered over the send button, then added:

"Not sure how long we'll stay. Hoping it's long enough."

She hit send, watching the bar spin for a moment before the message pushed through.

James sipped his coffee. "Sofia?"

Leena nodded. "She'd kill me if I didn't check in."

"Well its better to be safe."

They lapsed into a comfortable quiet as the song wound to an end. James tapped the table with his fingers.

"I used to dream about a place like this," he said. "Not the cabin or the break. Just… pulling off the road somewhere, eating pancakes with someone who doesn't hate me."

Leena looked at him, then at her coffee. "I don't hate you."

He smiled, eyes down. "That's a start."

Their food came. They ate slowly, like people rediscovering hunger. The diner hummed around them, and absolutely nothing felt like it needed fixing.

Eventually, they stood, paid, and stepped back into the cool evening air. The road waited. The store would come next.

James held the door open for her as they stepped out into the golden hour chill, it hinted at nightfall and promised a drop in temperature. They made their way back to the car, the scent of pine mingling now with the diner's lingering grease and syrup.

As James turned the key in the ignition, he glanced over. "You know, that might've been the most emotionally fulfilling pancake I've ever eaten."

Leena smirked. "Pancakes can fix things."

"That should be their slogan. 'Millie's: Come for the emotional breakdown, stay for the syrup.'"

She laughed lightly, then turned her head to watch the pines blur past again. The road twisted and narrowed, sending long shadows stretching across the pavement like ghosts.

"That song… I haven't heard it in years," she said suddenly. "It hit different today."

James nodded, keeping his eyes on the road. "You remember when we first moved in together, and we tried to dance in the kitchen? I kept stepping on your toes."

"You were a terrible dancer."

"Still am. But I remember thinking… If we ever had a real moment like a movie moment that would've been it."

Leena turned her face away, pretending to look out the window, but she didn't miss the crack in his voice. That old hurt was still there, but softened now, aged like the walls of the diner.

The map sat between them on the console, folded open to a page with a bold red circle scribbled around the name of a small town. James tapped it with his index finger. "We'll try there. Might be small, but I'm betting it has at least one store that carries toilet paper."

"And bacon. Don't forget bacon."

"I wouldn't dare."

They drove in silence for a while, the kind of silence that comes with comfort, not tension. The pines thinned slightly, revealing a valley stretched wide with patchy farmland small houses and an old gas station perched at the far corner. A rusted sign announced: "Tanner's Grocery – 1 Mile."

James raised an eyebrow. "Tanner's sounds like a place where the cashier might also be the mayor."

"Perfect," Leena said. "Maybe the mayor can direct us to the good tp".

They laughed again small, real laughs. And the road, for all its bends and dips, felt lighter beneath the tires. Like something old was beginning to lift.

The town of Tanner's Grove looked like it had been plucked straight from an old black-and-white film and set gently down in the middle of nowhere. The main street was no more than a single lane flanked by narrow sidewalks and vintage storefronts. Weathered brick buildings wore fading signs in hand-painted script: 'Antiques,' 'Birch & Bloom Florals,' and a barbershop with a spinning red-and-white pole that still turning reaping the nostalgia of a time gone by.

Window displays featured hand-knit scarves, vintage glassware, and chalkboards with quotes of the day scribbled in looping cursive. A golden retriever lay sleeping in the doorway of what appeared to be a bookstore and cafe.

The grocery store sat at the far end, a squat building with green awnings and ivy creeping up one side. Its sign read simply: 'Tanner's Grocery – Est. 1941.' The place had charm the kind of charm that didn't try too hard. A pair of old rocking chairs sat outside, one missing a slat, the other occupied by a scarecrow dressed in flannel and overalls.

Inside, the floors creaked underfoot and the air smelled faintly of wood polish, ripe fruit, and something warm and yeasty baking in the back. Shelves were lined with mismatched jars of preserves, hand-labeled with names like "Raspberry Thyme" and "Apple Chutney."

Leena pushed the cart while James trailed beside her, basket in hand. Locals moved slowly through the aisles friendly faces that didn't question their presence, just nodded with small-town courtesy.

"This is like a grocery store themed after a Hallmark movie," James whispered as they passed a display of maple syrup bottles shaped like leaves.

Leena chuckled. "Let's just hope they have what we need"

They rounded a corner and breathed a mutual sigh of relief at the sight of a well-stocked paper goods shelf.

"Hallelujah," James muttered, tossing a pack of the good toilet paper into the cart.

They moved through the store slowly, picking up pancake mix, syrup, and a few other essentials that wouldn't require a degree in culinary science. Every now and then, James would sneak something ridiculous into the cart a novelty-sized jar of pickles, off-brand cereal with cartoon aliens on the box just to see if she noticed. Leena did, and each time she'd toss it back onto the shelf with a playful glare.

She lingered near the checkout at a small rack of postcards, her fingers brushing over faded images of the lake and winding trails. It looked like the kind of town that existed just slightly out of step with the rest of the world.

James set the basket on the counter and gave a polite nod to the woman behind the register. Her name tag read 'Darla,' and she looked up from her crossword with a tired but knowing smile.

"Y'all here for one of the cabins?" She asked, scanning the items.

"Yeah," Leena said, adjusting the cart. "Just trying to keep it stocked with the basics."

Darla nodded. "Can't say I blame you. Town's small, but we've got what you need."

James raised an eyebrow. "Thank God. We were two pine needles away from a tragedy."

Darla snorted. "Been there."

Leena rolled her eyes, but her smirk showed her amusement."

As they stepped back outside, arms full of bags, the sun was starting to dip behind the trees, casting long shadows across the street. A breeze tugged at Leena's hair, and for a moment, it felt life was something slower. Simpler.

Back in the car, she looked over at James. "Weirdly, I didn't want to leave."

"Same," he said.

She smiled, and they drove back toward the cabin, the little town shrinking behind them like the closing page of a well-loved book. They drove in easy silence. The pine trees flanked them once more, the road curling gently like a path leading them back into their own story.

Back at the cabin, the air greeted them like an old friend cool and pine-sweet, carrying the hush of the lake and the rustle of the forest. James stepped out first, stretching his arms with a groan as the wind tugged gently at his jacket.

Leena followed, juggling two grocery bags and grinning as the screen door creaked open on its hinge. The inside welcomed them again warm and wood-scented, the fire still crackling faintly from earlier embers.

James set the bags down on the counter. "Okay," he said, rolling his shoulders. "We've got food, supplies, and enough toilet paper to last a small army."

Leena laughed, pulling the pancake mix from one of the bags. "Let's just hope this place has a whisk."

They moved together in rhythm, unpacking groceries, sharing quiet looks and small, incidental touches that carried more weight than either would admit. As the last bag was emptied and put away, James paused beside the record player, flipping through the vinyl collection.

"Music?" He asked.
Leena smiled. "Only if you find something without bagpipes."
He smirked and lifted a Sinatra album.

The cabin filled with the soft grain of old records as they stood side by side in the soft lamplight two people still tangled in the knots of their past, but inching forward, one quiet evening at a time.

Chapter 6

Later that night, the cabin was quiet. The lake barely moved, the trees stood still, and inside, the old wood creaked just enough to remind them they weren't alone in the silence. They had unpacked, settled in, and wandered a bit, and now came the unspoken part: deciding where to sleep.

They didn't discuss it. Two bedrooms meant two options, and maybe they were both too careful, too exhausted, to suggest anything else. Leena had taken the smaller room, James the one with the lake view.

It should've been easy to sleep. But of course, it wasn't.

Leena lay on her side, the quilt pulled high, eyes fixed on the wooden beams above. The stillness felt too loud. Too aware. The mattress creaked every time she moved, and the shadows on the walls seemed to shift with each blink. Her thoughts ran laps, dragging behind them the baggage they'd both sworn not to unpack yet.

She rolled onto her back, sighing. Her fingers drummed softly on the blanket, then paused. Somewhere down the hall, a floorboard creaked a normal cabin sound, but it made her heart race anyway. Not a scared race. Just from being alone.

Finally, she threw the covers back and stood, the floor cool beneath her feet. The hallway was dim, lit only by the faint glow spilling from the lamp in James's room. She stopped at his door, knuckles hovering midair. Then, gently, she knocked.

James stirred. He hadn't been asleep. "Yeah?"

"It's me," she said, voice low.

The door creaked open, and she stood there, arms wrapped around herself. "I can't sleep."

He stepped aside wordlessly and let her in.

The room smelled faintly of cedar and lake air. One bedside lamp was still on, casting a golden circle on the pine walls. James moved a book off the bed without comment. He'd only been pretending to read it anyway.

Leena sat on the edge of the mattress. "I thought I'd be tired enough to crash."

James nodded, standing a few feet away with his arms crossed loosely. "So did I."

They didn't look at each other immediately. The silence pressed in again, but it didn't have sharp edges. Just quiet acknowledgment.

"There's something weird about this place," Leena finally said.

"Weird bad or weird...?"

"Weird like..." She paused, searching. "Like it's pushing us together. Not in a creepy horror movie way. Just... Nudging."

James allowed himself a faint smile. "I've felt it too."

She turned toward him, pulling her legs up onto the bed. "It's like the air's too clean for resentment."

He sat down beside her slowly, careful not to crowd. "Might be the pine trees. I read somewhere they can boost your mood."

"Or it's haunted by really emotionally intelligent ghosts."

James huffed a quiet laugh. "That's a movie waiting to happen."

They sat in silence for a beat. Then another. Her shoulder brushed his.

"I'm sorry," he said, voice low. "For the way things were. For not seeing how far off track I'd gotten."

Leena didn't answer right away. But she didn't pull away.

"I think we both went blind," she said eventually. "Different reasons. Same result."

James nodded, the weight of her words hitting somewhere deep in his chest. "Yeah."

She glanced down at her hands, then at him. "You know, I used to think if we ever ended up in a place like this, it would be because we were happy. Because we wanted the same escape."

His voice was soft. "I wanted this even then. I just didn't know how to ask for it without it sounding like an apology."

They sat a while longer like that closer than before, but still unsure of the map forward. The room held its breath with them, the wind outside brushing against the window like a lullaby.

"You want me to go back to the other room?" She asked, not moving.

James shook his head. "Nope."

She shifted slowly under the covers, and after a moment, he did too. They lay there, not touching at first, then her head found the curve of his shoulder, and his arm wrapped around her out of instinct more than intent.

Her breath evened out gradually, soft and slow.

He stayed awake longer, staring at the ceiling, guilt curling quietly in the corners of his chest. She was here but so was everything they hadn't said. Still, in this strange cabin, in this strange silence, he let the guilt be what it was.

He listened to her breathing, slow and steady, and realized how long it had been since they'd fallen asleep this close. Her hand rested near his ribs, not quite holding on, but not letting go either.

In the dark, with her breath warming the hollow of his neck, James whispered into the quiet.

"Maybe we needed to fall apart to figure out what matters"

She didn't stir. But he liked to think, somehow, she heard it.

Tomorrow, they'd try again.

The lake would be waiting.

And maybe for the first time in a long time so would they.

James awoke to soft light seeping through the curtains. It filtered golden across the room, catching the dust motes that danced lazily in the still air. Leena was still tucked against him, her head resting on his chest now, one hand curled under her chin. The weight of her, light and warm, was strangely grounding.

He didn't move. Not for a while. Just watched the light change on the ceiling and listened to her breath.

Eventually, she stirred. Her lashes fluttered against his skin before her eyes opened, slow and unsure. There was a pause an invisible check-in with herself before she looked up at him.

"Morning," she whispered, voice scratchy.

"Hey," he said softly. "Sleep okay?"

She nodded. "Better than I expected."

He smoothed her hair back gently. "You were out."

She let out a sleepy laugh. "I think your heartbeat knocked me out. Like a metronome."

They didn't rush to move. It wasn't some grand romantic gesture it was just peace. The quiet didn't demand a reaction. Just two people, slowly existing near each other again.

Eventually, Leena sat up and stretched, her sweater slipping off one shoulder. "I feel like coffee would solve at least 70% of our problems right now."

James grinned. "And the other 30%?"

"Food. Obviously."

They both laughed tired, real laughter. And somehow, that was even better than sleep.

The morning at the cabin moved slow and unhurried. James brewed the coffee in the old percolator while Leena sifted through the dusty pantry to find a skillet and tried to coax the ancient gas stove to life. They bumped into each other in the tiny kitchen more than necessary, stealing glances, brushing hands.

By the time they sat down to eat, sunlight had filled the room, warming the knotty pine walls and glittering off the lake outside.

They didn't talk much while eating. But the silence wasn't loaded. Just comfortable.

Leena sipped her coffee and looked out the window. "So what do we do today?"

James leaned back in his chair, eyes on her. "Whatever we want."

She smiled.

It was a start.

After breakfast, they lingered at the table longer than necessary. James refilled their mugs and opened a few windows to let the lake air in. The breeze moved through the cabin, brushing against curtains and lifting the edge of a page in a magazine someone had left behind.

Leena tucked her feet up on the bench seat, her hair twisted into a loose knot. She watched the rippling surface of the lake through the glass, then turned to James. "I forgot what it feels like to not be on a schedule."

James leaned against the counter, sipping his coffee. "Same. It's like my brain keeps looking for something it should be doing."

She smirked. "Old habits."

He grinned and gestured toward the old record player in the corner. "Want to put something on?"

Leena nodded and stood. As she rifled through the stack of vinyls, she glanced over her shoulder. "How are you feeling about all this?"

He took a moment, then said, "Hopeful, but not scared. You?"

She found a Fleetwood Mac album and placed it on the turntable.

"The same. Except maybe more scared."

The needle dropped. The soft crackle of static and the opening chords of "Landslide" filled the space. James exhaled slowly and crossed the room to stand beside her.

The song played while they both looked out over the lake.

Neither of them said it, but they both felt it:

Something was changing.

The day was waiting.

James stood, stretching his arms above his head and cracking his neck. The cabin air smelled like warm pine, faintly sweet and rich with earth. Outside, the lake shimmered under the high sun, its surface broken only by the occasional ripple of wind. A small dock extended into the water like a punctuation mark at the edge of the woods.

Leena opened the front door and stepped out onto the porch, coffee mug in hand. The sunlight made her squint, and she tilted her face to it like a cat. "We should walk down to the lake," she said, not looking back.

"Yeah?"
"Feels like the kind of day that would be wasted otherwise."

James followed her outside, slipping on a hoodie and shoes. The porch steps creaked under their feet. The path to the lake was narrow and overgrown, covered with pine needles and framed by wild ferns. Birds chirped overhead like a living soundtrack. The smell of water grew stronger with every step.

When they reached the dock, Leena stopped short. "Wow," she breathed.

The lake was clearer than they'd realized, a mirror of sky and tree. It was quiet, except for the wind, and the occasional whisper of lapping water against the wooden planks.

She sat down at the edge, dipping her toes in and shivering. "Still cold."

James laughed and dropped beside her. "Give it another week."

They sat there in silence for a while, their shoulders brushing occasionally, neither pulling away.

"This place really is magical" Leena said softly.

James looked out over the lake. "Yeah, maybe it just reminds us who we used to be."

She glanced sideways at him. "You think we could get back there?"

He hesitated. "I don't know, maybe." "I think we could find something better. If we let it."

She nodded, staring out across the water like it held the answer.

Behind them, the cabin waited, windows glinting in the sunlight like blinking eyes. The day stretched wide before them like a blank page.

The breeze off the lake tugged gently at Leena's hair, and she closed her eyes for a long moment, breathing it in like it was something sacred. She could almost taste salt in the air, even though the lake wasn't anywhere near the ocean. Maybe it was just her mind, loosening its grip on the grind and starting to imagine again.

James glanced at her, watching the way the sunlight danced across her skin. "You okay?"

She opened her eyes and smiled. "Weirdly, yeah."

A bird call echoed across the water lonely and perfect.

They stayed there for a while, letting the world fall away. Every once in a while, one of them would start to say something, then just... Not. The quiet was too good to break without reason.

Eventually, Leena leaned back on her hands, squinting at the cloudless sky. "Do you remember that trip we took after college? The one where the car broke down outside Nashville and we ended up sleeping in the backseat with half a bag of pretzels?"

James chuckled. "You mean the one where you tried to fix the radiator with duct tape and your imagination?"

"Hey It worked!"

"Yeah for like twenty-seven miles."

She laughed. It was a sound that hadn't been easy to come by lately clear, surprised, unguarded. "That was a good trip, though."

"Yeah," he said. It was." "We didn't care about the world back then."

Leena looked down at the water again, her reflection wobbly and sunlit. "Maybe we still don't. Maybe its just different now."

James dipped his fingers into the lake and flicked water at her. "Still old and grumpy?"

She gasped and kicked a little water back at him with her toes. "Speak for yourself. I am a graceful woodland creature."

He smiled, wiping his face. "Who snores."

"I do not!"

They dissolved into laughter again. And when it faded, it left behind something lighter in its place.

After a long moment, Leena stood, brushing off the back of her jeans. "We should probably change. Maybe take a real walk? Explore the trail behind the cabin?"

James stood too. "Let's grab a camera. Just in case something photogenic happens."

She raised an eyebrow. "Like me falling on my ass again?"

He grinned. "Exactly that."

They made their way back up the path, a little slower, a little more in step. The cabin's porch came into view, it didn't feel like a retreat it felt like a beginning.

As they stepped onto the porch, Leena paused, her hand resting lightly on the railing. "I missed this," she said. "Not just the quiet. The... Feeling of nothing pulling us apart for a while."

James nodded. "It's like the world shut up long enough for us to hear each other again."

Inside, the cabin felt even warmer after their time at the lake. The wood creaked underfoot like a familiar rhythm, and the scent of pine and old stories lingered in every room. James grabbed the camera from his bag, checking the battery out of habit.

"You sure you're up for a hike?" He asked, slinging the strap over his shoulder.

Leena smirked. "What, are you worried?"

"Worried I'll have to carry you back and then listen to you mock me for how winded I get."

She nudged him with her shoulder. "Deal."

They followed the winding trail behind the cabin, where the trees grew denser and the light filtered through in shifting patterns. The world narrowed to the crunch of their steps and the occasional rustle of some unseen animal in the brush.

Along the way, Leena pointed out curious mushrooms and twisted tree trunks that looked like frozen dancers mid-pose. James snapped photos here and there not of sweeping landscapes, but the small things: her hand brushing a fern, her laughing profile framed in leaves.

When they stopped to catch their breath, Leena leaned against a mossy boulder. "You ever think about how easy this all feels now, compared to how hard we made it before?"

James looked at her. "Yeah. Like maybe we were trying too hard to fix the wrong things."

She nodded slowly. "I kept trying to build something on top of the cracks. Pretending they weren't there."

He stepped closer, brushing a leaf from her shoulder. "We both did. But maybe this time, we start from the ground. No pretending."

Leena met his eyes for a beat, the breeze catching her hair just so. Then she smiled, and something in his chest relaxed.

The trail curved back toward the lake, the sound of water growing louder as they walked. By the time they returned to the cabin, the sun was leaning westward, casting long shadows across the porch.

They sat side by side on the steps, the camera resting between them,

And as the light faded, they stayed like that quiet, but not distant.

Leena reached down to pick up a pine cone at her feet, turning it slowly in her hands like she was trying to read a story hidden in the spirals. James watched her, then turned his gaze back to the lake. The surface was starting to ripple now, a gentle wind brushing through the valley.

"What if we don't go back?" She said, still looking at the pine cone.

James blinked. "Home?"

"To all of it. The schedules. The white noise. The walking-on-egg-shells part of our lives."

He considered it. Not as a fantasy, but as something that, in the right light, could be real.

"We'd need jobs," he said eventually.

"We'd need each other more," she countered, quiet but sure.

They both laughed, not because it was a joke, but because it was terrifying.

The kind of laugh that comes with the edge of something unspoken.

James stood and dusted off his jeans. "Come on. Let's go inside before one of the mosquitoes decide to tell the rest."

Leena followed, slower, but with a lighter step. Inside, the cabin welcomed them with the creak of its floorboards and the scent of old paper and pine.

James reached for the record player again. "Same album?"

Leena nodded. "Yeah. Let it play."

The vinyl hissed to life. Familiar chords filled the space.

And when the song reached the line about seasons of change and getting older, neither of them looked away.

Outside, the sun had all but gone, shadows stretching like ink across the lake.

Inside, they didn't feel like people waiting to leave.

They felt like people who had just arrived.

James glanced at her with a slow smile. "Want to make dinner together?"

Leena arched an eyebrow, amused. "You mean, you want me to supervise while you try to chop vegetables with the precision of a blindfolded amputee?"

He held up his hands. "I'll try not to lose a finger."

She smirked. "Alright, chef. Let's do it."

They moved easily in the small kitchen, the kind of dance only people with years of quiet familiarity could pull off. He stirred a pot of pasta while she chopped garlic with exaggerated care, mocking his earlier attempts. She reached over now and then to add herbs or nudge him aside with her hip.

"What are we calling this?" James asked, peering into the pot.

"Hopeless Cabin Pasta," she declared.

"That sounds like it comes with a side of cliche."

She laughed. "Only if it's served with candlelight."

Minutes later, they lit the candles leftover from whoever stocked the cabin last, setting them in empty wine bottles. The table was small but warm, bathed in golden light from both the flames and the lingering glow outside the windows. They sat across from each other, feet brushing under the table like teenagers playing a secret game.

"This is good," she said between bites.
He raised his glass. "To edible mistakes."

After dinner, they moved in tandem to clean up, bumping into each other again in that way that wasn't quite accidental. James rinsed the dishes as Leena dried them.

As he stood at the sink, scrubbing the last plate, she crossed the room quietly, thumbing through the stack of records again. She found one she hadn't noticed earlier Harry James and His Orchestra. She slid it from its sleeve and smiled to herself at the track list.

She smiled as she placed the record on the player and dropped the needle.

The soft, wistful notes of "It's Been a Long, Long Time" floated through the cabin.

James paused mid-rinse. His head turned slightly, recognizing the song before a smile tugged at his lips.

Leena approached, hands behind her back. "Captain," she said with a mock-serious nod. "Care to dance?"

James turned slowly, drying his hands on his jeans. "I'll try my best"

She stepped close, slipping her hands into his. "We'll try to figure it out together.

James gently pulled her closer, their fingers interlacing like two old pages sewn together in the same book. The worn wooden floor beneath them groaned softly in approval, as if recognizing the weight of the moment. They stood still at first, barely swaying, more an embrace than a dance.

His hand settled on the small of her back, the warmth of her body grounding him in a way he hadn't felt quite sometime. Leena laid her head lightly on his shoulder, letting her eyes drift closed, letting the music hold her in place as much as James did. The soft trumpet, nostalgic and aching, filled the cabin like perfume from another decade.

James didn't rush. He moved with the rhythm, slow and steady, every step considered. Not just because he didn't want to step on her, but because something about the moment deserved it. He found himself remembering the first time he saw her dance drunk off laughter at a college party, spinning barefoot in someone's living room. Carefree in a way he hadn't seen in a long time.

Leena's breath moved against his neck, soft and deliberate. She didn't speak, but he could feel it the way she pressed just slightly closer. The way her fingers flexed every now and then against his.

The cabin seemed to shrink around them, the walls no longer wood but memory and breath and possibility. The song didn't just play it reached into them, pulled up the things they didn't know they'd buried. The quiet forgiveness. The tentative hope. The ache of still wanting each other.

They didn't speak because they didn't need to.

James held her a little tighter and closed his eyes, resting his cheek against her hair. He let himself feel it. All of it. The guilt, the regret, the want. And the fragile thread of something else, something newer.

Not redemption.

When the song ended, they stayed wrapped together, unmoving. The needle hissed against the vinyl in soft static, and still neither of them pulled away.

Just because the music had stopped but because it hadn't ended in them yet.

James's hand drifted to Leena's waist, her breath catching slightly as he leaned in. There was no rush, no desperation just a heat that rose slowly, earnestly, like a tide between two people who had almost forgotten the shape of each other's bodies.

She tilted her head up, their eyes meeting. No words passed, just shared understanding, deep and slow-burning. A beat, then another, and then their mouths met with the soft reverence of remembering. Her hands curled into the fabric of his shirt, his arms tightening around her in reply.

They backed toward the couch, kissing between half-laughed whispers, as clothes were shed like old armor. The low creak of the floorboards punctuated their slow descent into something tender and familiar yet made new by absence, by time, by the sheer fragility of the moment.

They tumbled gently onto the couch, limbs tangled, breathless. Her fingers brushed the scar just beneath his collarbone one she'd always touched absentmindedly, but now did with purpose. He traced the freckle on her shoulder, the one that looked like a tiny star.

She broke the kiss, looking at him. "Are we doing this because we're here… or because we're us?"

James didn't flinch. "Because I still see you. Even when it's dark."

She nodded, pulled him back in.

They shifted again, rising clumsily from the couch, kissing and bumping into the narrow hallway wall in the process. James laughed, a real laugh that hadn't come from him in what felt like months. Leena's smile was soft and electric.

By the time they made it into the bedroom, moonlight had spilled across the sheets, the record long since turned to static.

They didn't rush. It wasn't about escaping anything it was about choosing to stay.

The quiet that followed wasn't awkward it was sacred. A hush full of meaning, their bodies tangled in a way that didn't demand more, just allowed presence. They held each other as if trying to memorize the shape of what forgiveness might feel like.

The open window let in the cool hush of night, and James listened to the rhythm of her breathing, anchoring him. He wanted to believe they could build something again beside what had been, like planting something new in soil they'd both turned over with their own hands.

He pressed his lips to her forehead, lightly. A whisper of a promise he hadn't figured out the words for yet.

For a time in what felt like years, his thoughts weren't filled with ways to fix things they were filled with moments like this. Quiet, close, but more importantly undeniably human.

He wondered if that was the point all along not to solve the puzzle, but to hold the broken pieces together long enough to see what could still shine through the cracks.

They breathed in sync, a slow lullaby in the dark.

And when he finally closed his eyes, it wasn't with guilt. It was with hope.

Later, wrapped in sheets and silence, Leena traced lazy circles on his chest, her cheek pressed against him. James stared at the ceiling, every breath slow and deliberate.

She murmured, "Something about this place…"

He kissed the top of her head. "Yeah. It lets you remember what matters."

Chapter 7

James woke before Leena again, the soft rustle of pine needles in the wind barely filtering through the cabin's windows. He lay still for a while, just watching the lazy spin of dust motes in the sunbeams streaking across the ceiling. Her head rested against his shoulder, her breath warm against his skin. It should've felt strange, waking up beside her again after so long but it didn't. It felt natural, like a rhythm remembered after forgetting the melody.

Eventually, he slipped out of bed quietly, careful not to wake her. In the kitchen, he brewed coffee and started prepping pancake batter. By the time the aroma reached the bedroom, Leena stirred, blinking against the soft morning light. She walked out wearing one of his old shirts, sleeves hanging long over her hands, her hair a tousled mess that somehow made her look more herself than she had in weeks.

"You're cooking?" She said, rubbing one eye.

"Only the greatest breakfast food ever invented."

She snorted. "Coffee first. Praise later."

They moved around each other with the ease of shared space passing ingredients, dodging elbows, teasing. It was quiet but warm, and the pancakes were golden and slightly uneven, just the way she liked them.

As they ate, James leaned back in his chair and sighed. "We're going to need to hit the store again."

Leena raised an eyebrow. "Already planning your next culinary disaster?"

"Absolutely. But also, if we want to avoid rationing coffee and pretending stale crackers are gourmet, we should probably stock up. Enough for the rest of the week."

She nodded, sipping her mug. "Same town?"

She stood and stretched. "I should check in again once I get service. Let Sofia know we're still alive."

James chuckled. "She still your emergency contact?"

"She's my 'I told you so' accountability partner."

They cleaned up quickly, throwing on layers and grabbing their now-familiar printed map. The drive back into town was peaceful, winding through pine-laced roads that curved like old songs. The sun filtered through the trees in slanted rays, dappling the hood of the car.

They arrived and decided to take their time. They wandered past shop windows filled with odds and ends, through the scent of an open bakery door.

Eventually, the diner's red neon sign glowed faintly in the midday light. Inside, the same checkered floor, same red vinyl booths welcomed them. A few locals nodded, familiar but uninterested in small talk.

They slid into the same booth by the window and ordered burgers and fries. It felt like something settled into place.

Halfway through the meal, the jukebox kicked on again.

The opening notes of that song floated out, warm and sweet.

Leena paused mid-bite and looked at James. "You're kidding."

He held up his hands. "I swear I didn't plan that."

She shook her head with a soft smile. "This place has a sense of humor."

He leaned back, savoring the song. "You know, when Cap finally got his dance with Peggy at the end of Endgame, I remember thinking... Damn. That's the kind of peace you only get after hell."

Leena gave him a look. "You're comparing us to Captain America and Peggy?"

"Why not?" James grinned. "I finally got my Peggy. Took me long enough."

She reached across the table and lightly tapped his hand. "Don't screw it up, Rogers."

"I'll do my best, Carter."

They laughed again this time it felt earned

After lunch, they strolled briefly, then headed to the small grocery store. It was the kind of place where the aisles were narrow and every item had a story. They didn't rush browsing shelves, comparing labels, tossing things into the cart with little jokes along the way.

More toilet paper, of course, was top of the list.

James held up a pack like a trophy. "Victory is ours."

Leena added it to the cart with a grin.
They filled their cart with simple food, enough to last them until it was time to go.

Nothing fancy just the basics, things they'd actually eat, things that would remind them of this odd little retreat.

Once outside, they loaded the bags into the trunk. Leena checked her phone as notifications started coming through.

She tapped out a message to Sofia: "Still alive. Still here. I'll drop a pin when we're closer to the cabin in case it all implodes."

Sofia replied almost instantly: "Rooting for you. Don't do anything stupid."

Leena smiled and tucked the phone away.

James looked over as he started the car. "Ready?"

"Yeah," she said. "Let's go home."

The road wound back through the trees, sunlight flickering through the leaves like applause.

And this time, the silence between them didn't ask questions, it answered them.

Back at the cabin, Leena stood by the window for a long moment after they'd brought the groceries in, her eyes following the gentle ripple of the lake. The air had that early evening hush to it thick with pine and stillness, as if the world was pausing just for them.

She moved quietly to the corner of the cabin where she'd stashed her art supplies in a beat-up canvas tote. It had been a while. Too long, maybe. But her fingers still itched for brushes and color. She unpacked her easels, tubes of oil paint, a palette with dried memories stuck to its edges.

James watched from the couch, his arm draped over the backrest, a soft smile playing at his lips.

"You going to go paint?"

She nodded, unrolling a long sheet of thick paper. "I think this place is telling me to."

He leaned forward. "Do you know what?"

Leena looked out the window again. "Not yet. But it's not about knowing. It's about starting."

She set up near the open window where the golden light spilled across the hardwood floor, brushing a lock of hair behind her ear as she mixed colors on instinct alone. The scent of lilac oil mingled with the wood and fresh air, something ancient and new wrapped together.

Outside, a breeze moved the trees gently. Inside, the quiet turned into something sacred again brushes against canvas, the occasional shift of her weight on the stool, James flipping pages in a book he wasn't reading, watching her more than the text.

Neither said much.
They didn't need to.

Leena's brush moved in fluid strokes, her focus narrowed in on the page. Color flowed into shapes that hadn't yet decided what they wanted to be just bursts of emotion, light, and texture. Her brow furrowed slightly as she worked, but her lips twitched with a quiet satisfaction. It wasn't about the final image. It was the act of doing it.

James stayed silent, letting the rhythm of her painting set the tone for the cabin. He found himself watching her hands the way they moved with purpose and softness all at once. There was grace in the mess she was making.

After a while, she broke the silence.

"I forgot what this felt like."

"Creating?"

She nodded. "Yeah, without pressure. Without trying to prove something to anyone. Just… painting because I want to."

James shifted on the couch, resting his chin on his hand. "This place kind of strips the world away. It just leaves us."

She didn't answer right away, just dipped her brush into another color. "Maybe that's what we needed. To lose the world for a little while."

Outside, the lake glimmered like liquid glass. Somewhere, a bird called in the distance. The fire in the hearth had dwindled to glowing embers, casting a golden hue over the wooden walls.

Leena stood and stepped back from the easel, smudging paint on her shirt as she crossed her arms. James got up and walked over, standing behind her.

The canvas was still abstract, but something about it. Like a storm breaking open to reveal the light behind it.

"It's beautiful," he said quietly.

She glanced over her shoulder. "It's not even close to anything."

"I didn't say it needed to be."
They just stood there, side by side.
Finally the quiet didn't ache It breathed.

James stepped away quietly, drawn to the low shelf near the fireplace where a stack of weathered books rested beneath an old brass lamp. His fingers skimmed the spines, pausing on a faded cloth-bound volume titled Whispers from the Pines: A Local History.

He brought it to the armchair and opened it, the binding crackling softly in protest. The pages were yellowed, edges curled, but the text was still sharp typed on an old machine, scattered with penciled margin notes.

The first chapter was simple how the lake had once been a sacred gathering spot for indigenous tribes, revered as a place where the veil between worlds thinned in the mist. Stories of healers and vision-seekers filled those early pages.

James turned another page, eyebrows lifting as he read an entry about where the cabin itself stood, It had once been part of a small retreat used by artists and musicians in the 1940s, drawn by the seclusion. Some of them had gone on to become minor legends in their own circles painters whose brushstrokes hung in obscure galleries, songwriters whose melodies were sampled decades later.

Further in, he came across a strange story about a couple who had vanished nearby in the 1970s. Their canoe had been found on the far side of the lake, undisturbed, their picnic blanket still laid out on the rocks. Locals swore the pair had simply walked into the woods and never returned, despite extensive searches. No signs. No struggles. Just... Gone.

Leena noticed the shift in his expression and lowered her brush.

"What's got you looking like you've seen a ghost?"

James held up the book, flipping it to the marked passage. "This place has some serious folklore. Artists going off-grid, mysterious disappearances, sacred water. Makes our trip feel like a rite of passage."

She set her palette down and walked over, peering at the page.

"Maybe we're just the next chapter."

He met her eyes, something both amused and thoughtful sparking between them. "Let's hope we don't vanish into the woods, though."

"No promises," she teased, nudging him with her shoulder.

James grinned and leaned back into the chair, still flipping through the book, his curiosity pulling him deeper into the pages. Leena returned to her canvas, but her strokes were slower now, more deliberate as if the cabin, the lake, and the stories whispered into her art.

Outside, the wind picked up just slightly, rippling across the lake like secrets being passed from tree to tree.

Inside the cabin, James read deeper into the book, the tales becoming more haunting and strange. He came across a chapter titled "Echoes of the Pines," which detailed local accounts of travelers who claimed to hear voices in the wind soft murmurs that seemed to call them by name. Skeptics dismissed them as tricks of the breeze, but others swore it felt like something ancient lingered in the woods, listening.

One account described an elderly woman who had lived in the area her most of her life. She claimed the lake had moods, that it mirrored the emotions of those who stayed too long. When she was sad, the water turned still and somber. When she laughed, the surface danced with wind even on windless days.

James felt a chill, not from the surreal poetry of it all. He looked up at Leena, now deep in her painting again, the light catching the side of her face as if the universe had picked just the right angle to remember her by. Her hair glowed in the gold fading through the window, her brush moving with rhythm, with trust.

A gust of wind swept around the cabin, shaking the trees just enough to make the pine needles hiss. James closed the book slowly, resting it on his lap as he stared into the flickering fire.

He wondered not aloud, not even in full thought if maybe the stories weren't just old myths. Maybe this place really did remember. Maybe the trees did whisper. Maybe some homes weren't built with wood and nails, but with memory.

And maybe, it had been waiting for them to return.

As the sun dipped lower, casting shadows that stretched across the wooden floor, Leena stood and stretched, her back arching with a soft pop. "You made breakfast," she said, glancing toward James. "That means dinner's on me."

He looked up from the fire, his smile easy. "Deal. Just don't burn the cabin down."

She shot him a playful glare and headed into the small kitchen. The air grew rich with the scent of sauteing onions and something vaguely garlicky. James wandered in to help but was quickly waved off.

"Sit. Relax," she insisted. "This one's mine."

He returned to the couch, watching her move with quiet confidence. It wasn't fancy pasta tossed with roasted vegetables and Parmesan but it smelled like comfort. Like care. Like love disguised in butter and salt.

They ate at the small kitchen table by the window, a single candle flickering between them. Outside, the lake shimmered in moonlight. Inside, time slowed down.

Conversation drifted lazily books, music, memories of better days. There were pauses, but they weren't empty. Just space for breathing, and looking, for remembering how to be near each other.

After the dishes were done, Leena leaned against the counter, arms crossed, watching James dry the last of the plates. He caught her gaze, and something unspoken passed between them ease, gratitude, something softer beneath the surface.

She moved to the small table and lit another candle, the warm glow bouncing off the walls. James joined her, both of them sitting in the quiet hush far removed from the noise of the world.

Their conversation wandered through childhood stories, old dreams, books half-finished and places never visited. James spoke of a time he'd almost moved to Portland for a job that would've kept him on the road. Leena confessed she'd once planned to live abroad for a year, but fear had kept her grounded.

It wasn't dramatic or emotional it was honest. Steady. The kind of connection that builds from declarations, but from attention. From care.

She leaned her head against his shoulder as the candlelight flickered between them. He didn't move, just let the moment rest. Somewhere in the stillness, it became clear they didn't have to say how much they loved each other.

He turned slightly, brushing her hair back from her face. Her eyes met his, something vulnerable and wanting flickering there. A breath passed between them no rush, no expectation, just gravity pulling one toward the other.

She leaned up and kissed him, slow and with meaning. There was nothing frantic this time. No apology, no guilt just heat that built like a tide. They moved to the couch, lips finding familiar places, hands rediscovering old maps of each other.

Clothing was shed in silence, each piece a layer of distance peeled away. The couch groaned beneath them, but they didn't care. The only sound was breath, and whispered names.

It wasn't just passion. It was hunger laced with memory the kind of closeness they hadn't dared to imagine in months. Every touch was a question and an answer all at once: Are we still here? Do we still know how to love like this?

And they did.

Afterward, she lay draped over him, her body tucked into the curve of his like a piece that had always belonged there. Her breathing slowed, deepened. She murmured something sleepy he couldn't quite catch, then slipped into slumber.

James stayed awake, his fingers brushing lightly along her back, memorizing the shape of her again. Guilt still sat with him, a quiet ghost in the corner the only difference was it didn't weigh as heavily

He stared at the ceiling for a while, letting the rhythm of her breathing settle into his chest. Eventually, eyes heavy, heart full and aching, he let sleep take him too.

Chapter 8

James woke to the low rumble of thunder. It hadn't been long maybe a couple of hours since they'd drifted off. The room was still dim, the morning light barely a suggestion behind the clouds. Rain tapped against the cabin's windows in a quiet rhythm, steady but gentle, a gray mist hanging just beyond the glass.

He blinked and realized the storm must have rolled in during the night. Leena was still curled against him on the couch, her cheek pressed to his chest, her hair a tumble of warmth and sleep. The blanket had slipped down around her waist, one of his arms still wrapped protectively around her.

He didn't want to move. Didn't want to lose this moment, this peace.

But the couch wasn't exactly forgiving.

He shifted slightly, brushing a kiss to the top of her head. "Hey," he whispered. "It's storming. Come on let's get into a real bed."

She mumbled something incoherent against his chest.

"What's that?"

Her voice was thick with sleep. "Carry me."

He chuckled softly. "You think I won't?"

A sleepy smile tugged at her lips. "You're all talk."

Challenge accepted.

James eased out from beneath her. She groaned at the shift, but didn't open her eyes. With exaggerated slowness, he tucked one arm beneath her knees, the other beneath her shoulders, and lifted her off the couch.

She gasped, laughing as her arms flailed and looped around his neck. "James! You're insane."

"You asked," he said, carrying her like a bride across the threshold. "I deliver."

"Put me down before you throw your back out."

"Then you'd have to carry me."

She snorted. "Romantic AND manipulative."

The bedroom was still warm from the night before, the covers slightly rumpled from their earlier sleep. He set her down gently onto the bed, and she immediately curled into the pillows like a cat claiming its territory.

James slipped in beside her. The storm hummed outside, slow and unhurried. Inside, there was only the soft rise and fall of their breathing and the occasional crackle of rain against the roof.

Leena peeked one eye open. "You're staying, right?"

He nodded, brushing a strand of hair off her forehead. "Nowhere else I'd rather be."

She smiled, eyes closing again, and within moments, her breathing evened out into sleep.

James listening to the storm, the steady rhythm of her breath, and the way the world had grown quiet around them.

It felt like the universe was exhaling.

So was he. Almost like the world they came from was just a clouded memory, the guilt seemed like just a mist no longer weighing him down but hovering faintly, barely there.

Finally, he was home. Not in the sense of walls or roofs, in the steady presence of the woman beside him. She was his home. All he had ever wanted since the first time he laid eyes on her before the bitterness, before everything that had cracked and splintered them holding her like this. To be worthy of it. And now, in the quiet pat of rain and second chances, he truly hoped he was.

Later, as the storm began to wane and the morning crept forward, James stirred beneath the covers. The space beside him was empty, the sheets still warm where Leena had been. His brow furrowed as his hand instinctively reached across the mattress, finding nothing but rumpled linen. A flicker of unease sparked in his chest an old reflex, the echo of too many mornings waking up alone.

He sat up slowly, eyes scanning the soft light that spilled through the curtains. The room was still, the storm outside reduced to a lazy drizzle.

Then he caught it the scent of coffee wafting through the hallway. Rich and inviting. Not burnt or bitter, but warm and familiar. The kind she always made, the kind he never quite got right.

His lips lifted in a sleepy smile.

She was still here.

And somehow, just knowing that feeling her presence in the scent of morning and the hush of rain settled something deep inside him.

By the time he stepped out of the bedroom, the drizzle had softened into a faint mist, and the sky was a pale, moody gray. Leena was nowhere inside the cabin, but a glance through the back window revealed her on the dock, seated cross-legged with a canvas propped in front of her. The lake stretched out calm and silver, a mirror for the sky. She painted slowly, deliberately, the colors of the water and trees forming beneath her brush.

James poured himself a cup of coffee, savoring its warmth as he leaned against the door frame to watch her. There was something sacred about the way she moved out there focused, almost reverent as if the quiet of the morning had infused itself into her strokes.

He walked down the worn steps, coffee still in hand, and joined her on the edge of the dock.

"You're up early," he said softly.

She glanced at him, eyes soft. "The lake was calling."

He nodded, settling beside her without another word, watching the way the sky met the water in long, slow lines.

For a while, they just sat there. No rush. There was no pressure. Just healing.

After a few minutes, James stood up stretched and said "I think I'll take a walk. Leave you to your masterpiece."

Leena looked up at him with a knowing smile. "Don't get lost."

"I won't go far. Just need to stretch my legs and maybe my thoughts."

She nodded and returned to her work, dipping her brush again.

James wandered off into the woods that wrapped around the cabin, letting the trail pull him forward. The air was thick with pine and damp earth, that scent that grounded you. Each step felt like a step away from the chaos they had left behind and toward something simpler.

They were healing. Not just as a couple, but as individuals, personally he felt as if for the first time in forever there was absolute peace.

As James moved deeper into the woods, the soft hush of mist and leaves seemed to invite reflection. The trail wasn't marked, he wasn't looking for a destination. Just distance, maybe. Space to unravel thoughts that had been coiled up too long.

The stillness of the forest gave him the silence to remember.

It wasn't just the fights or the cold nights or the betrayal that had fractured them. It had started long before that quietly, like all painful things do. The miscarriage. That word alone still felt heavy in his chest.

They had never really talked about it. Not properly. Not deeply. At the time, Leena had curled inward, closing herself off in a way that was subtle but absolute. Her grief had been vast, consuming, and James hadn't known how to reach her through it. He didn't process it. He had waited, grown silent, then resentful, and lonely.

And that loneliness had led to weakness. A moment, a mistake,a choice.

He hated himself for it.

But as the wind stirred the canopy above him and light filtered through the trees in fractured gold, he realized something else he hadn't known how to grieve either. They'd both broken in their own ways, and instead of holding each other through it, they had drifted apart
That unspoken truth had lived like a ghost between them for years. They'd tiptoe around it, pretend it hadn't happened, focus on anything else just to avoid that pain.

But out here, with the world stripped quiet and nothing to hide behind, James could see it clearly that was the wound they'd never dressed. The place they stopped being a team.

And now, finally, it was time to talk about it. To bring the silence into the light.

He didn't know how, but he knew it had to happen.

If they were really going to find their way back not just to each other, but to themselves it would have to start with the truth.

James sank onto a moss-covered rock just off the path, elbows resting on his knees, fingers like a steeple beneath his chin. The forest held its breath around him, hushed and listening. The silence pressed in not uncomfortably, but expectant. Like it was waiting for him to admit something.

He turned it over in his head again and again: how to bring it up. Or if he even should. What if it opened everything back up? What if the healing unraveled at the first mention of their loss? But then again… what if it was the only way forward?

A sigh escaped him.

Then, something caught his eye a narrow, overgrown path leading off the main trail, half-swallowed by brambles, tucked deeper into the woods than the rest. His curiosity flared. He tore a bit of the old receipt still in his pocket and tied it around a nearby branch, marking the trail for later. Just in case.

He stood slowly, the weight of the past still lingering in his chest, and began a slow walk deeper into the forest.

Out on the dock, Leena's brush hovered midair, unmoving.

She hadn't put anything new on the canvas in several minutes. The scene before her the silver lake, the sleepy sky blurred with memory.

It had started the same place his thoughts had gone.

The miscarriage.

She hadn't spoken of it aloud in years. It was a wound sealed with silence, too raw to poke at, too tangled to explain. She had turned inward to survive it, pulling into herself so tightly she left no room for James. And maybe she'd thought he would come find her in that place. Maybe she thought he'd understand without words.

But he hadn't. And her pain had become isolation. His silence had turned into distance. And somewhere in the chasm between them, they'd both lost sight of what they were.

She blinked back tears, brushing her thumb along the wood of the easel. Was it her fault? Had she shut him out too much? Had she knocked over the first domino?

"No," her inner voice whispered. "It was both of you."

But guilt didn't listen to reason.

The breeze pulled at her hair as she looked out across the lake. The silence between them, that ghost they both tiptoed around it was time to name it. Maybe not today. Maybe not even tomorrow. But soon.

Because no healing could truly last if they didn't go back to the moment the cracks began to form, forgive themselves for bleeding through them.

Her thoughts lingered there, wrapped in the hush of the lake and the brush of breeze across her skin. This trip it had started as an escape. A desperate Hail Mary pass. But it was turning into something else. Something gentler. Something almost magical. She didn't trust it yet. Didn't trust herself to believe in good things anymore. But there was a flicker of something stirring inside her.

Could it really be this simple? This beautiful?

She shook her head slightly and packed up her brushes, walking slowly back toward the cabin.

Inside, she set the canvas down on the small table by the door and wandered into the kitchen, the warmth of the wooden floors grounding her. She didn't know what time it was, it didn't matter.

Her fingers moved on instinct, pulling a pan from the cabinet, slicing a tomato, warming oil. She flipped on the old record player out of habit and chose something familiar Fleetwood Mac. The opening chords of "Landslide" spilled through the room, soft and melancholic.

She stirred onions in the pan, the scent rising like memory. As the lyrics echoed through the space, she caught her reflection in the window over the sink. Same eyes, maybe softer now. Same mouth, only less guarded.

Was she changing too?

The song played on while she cooked, her mind drifting. How could they talk about it? Could they? Would it hurt more than it healed?

Out in the woods, James walked the winding trail slowly, as if each step might unlock a piece of himself he hadn't touched in years.

The forest whispered with age, old secrets tangled in branches and moss. It felt like walking through memory unfiltered and bare.

He found a log near a bend in the trail and sat, elbows on his knees, the echo of Leena's laughter in his mind. He wondered if she was thinking the same things.

He wondered if she could forgive him.

More importantly if he could forgive himself.

A stick cracked and tumbled from the canopy above, landing with a dull thud in front of his boots. James blinked, glancing upward as if expecting the forest to give him another sign. But what caught his attention wasn't in the trees.

Beyond the curtain of ferns and moss, half-hidden by ivy and the curve of the slope, stood another cabin.

It was older, smaller tucked deep enough into the woods that you'd miss it if you weren't already lost in thought. Weather-worn wood, a sagging roof line, and a chimney crooked like a question mark. Still, it had presence, like it had grown there with the trees instead of being built. A place that had stories.

James stood slowly, heart thrumming for reasons he couldn't explain. He moved closer, cautious but drawn forward by something more than curiosity. Maybe it was the same thing that had led him here at all a need to unearth the past, to find where the threads first frayed.

He didn't step inside. Not yet. Just stood there, staring at the door like it might open by itself.

A chill passed through him not fear, but admiration. This place felt sacred in a strange, forgotten kind of way, like memory lived here, just waiting.

He turned back, noting the trail, his pulse still soft in his ears.

Whatever this place was, it mattered.

Chapter 9

James stood still in the forest clearing, heart still thrumming from the discovery of the old cabin. He didn't turn back toward their place. Not yet. Instead, he scanned the woods around him, thinking fast.

If he left now, he might not find this place again. The forest had a way of rearranging itself, of swallowing trails in a maze of green. So he began to work.

He dragged fallen branches across the moss, arranging them like crude arrows pointing toward the cabin. Then he stacked small cairns balanced piles of rock, one on top of the other at every fork in the trail and bend in the path. He used bark, twisted twigs into markers, and even scratched a shallow arrow into the earth with a pointed stick.

Each marker was small but intentional. Each one whispered: this way.

He lost track of time in the ritual of it, the careful placing of direction in a world that so often felt chaotic. There was something meditative in it something steady. When he finally looked up, the light had shifted, golden now and breaking through the thinning clouds.

Only then did he turn back, following his own trail through the trees, the image of the hidden cabin etched deep into his memory. Whatever was inside it whatever it meant it wasn't meant to be explored alone.

Not this time.

"Everything okay?" She asked, eyes catching his a beat too long.

"Yeah," he said, smiling.

Later, over lunch, he nearly told her. Almost reached across the table to say, "There's something I want to show you." But the words stayed behind his teeth, waiting for the right breath, the right hour.

Because when they stepped over that threshold into that cabin that seemed to live outside of time he wanted it to be together.

Not as broken people looking for answers.

But as a couple brave enough to face whatever they might find.

James watched her smile down at her phone screen, even though he knew she had no service out here. She wasn't reading a text maybe just an old photo or a saved note. The way her eyes crinkled, her shoulders relaxed, it stirred something in him deeper than memory. It wasn't the giddy spark of new love. It was something earned something weathered by storms.

He didn't want to shatter the delicate peace blooming between them with the weight of the past, not yet. But soon. Maybe tonight. Maybe after they took another walk, made another meal, curled up beside the fire again.

She looked at him then, as if sensing his thoughts. Her smile faded into something quieter, more thoughtful. She didn't say anything. She didn't need to.

They both knew there were things left to say.

But for in what felt like years, there was no fear in the knowing.

James reached across the table, fingers brushing hers. She met him halfway, her thumb tracing a circle across his knuckles. They didn't break eye contact. Didn't speak.

The silence said it all: We're still here. We're not done. We can do this.

The wind rattled the windowpanes softly, as if to remind them that outside, the world would keep on turning.

But in here, just for now, time belonged to them.

Laughter began to replace silence as they lingered at the table. James made a joke about the way she always cut tomatoes "surgical, like you're prepping them for a press conference."

She rolled her eyes but grinned, firing back something about his hopelessly uneven toast slices from breakfast. They bantered like that for a while, the kind of back-and-forth that had once been a daily rhythm, long before things had gotten so hard.

They migrated to the couch, wine glasses in hand, the afternoon light softening through the curtains. He told her a story from college she'd never heard before one about him dressing as a traffic cone for Halloween and getting hit on by a very confused drunk guy in a banana suit. She laughed so hard she had to set her glass down.

Then came the quiet again. Not strained, just full. Full of unsaid things, of promises not yet spoken, of a deep and aching love that hadn't died only gotten lost.

She set her glass aside and leaned into him, and he wrapped his arms around her without needing to be asked. There was no hesitation now. No shame, no past clawing its way into the room. Just skin on skin, breath against breath, the slow rediscovery of something that had always been there beneath the wreckage.

They made love again with a kind of sacred slowness, an unspoken apology in every touch. It was tender, and honest, and more vulnerable. There were no words during, only soft gasps, trembling sighs, and the occasional laugh muffled against a shoulder.

Later, tangled together in the warm quiet, Leena ran her fingers along his chest and whispered, "This feels like us again."

James kissed her forehead and held her tighter. "I really think because it is."

They lay in a loose tangle for a while, bodies warm and breathing slowly syncing, his hand resting lightly on the curve of her back. The world outside hummed with cicadas and late summer air, thick with the scent of pine and earth.

"We should probably figure out dinner," she murmured eventually, her voice still drowsy and sweet.

He chuckled. "You reading my mind again?"

"Always," she said, then propped herself up slightly. "We could cook... Or we could head back into town."

James raised a brow. "Back to the diner? I wouldn't say no to round two of that pie."

She grinned. "I was hoping you'd say that."

They slowly got dressed, stealing kisses between clothing changes, joking about who got ready faster. As she pulled her hair into a loose knot, Leena glanced at him through the mirror. "Might be nice to walk around a little. Window shop. See if that quirky little bookstore is open."

"Deal. But only if I get to pick the music on the way."

"We're not listening to your epic space metal playlist again, James."

"Come on," he groaned dramatically. "It's emotionally complex."

She laughed. "It's dragons in space screaming to guitar solos."

"Exactly. Art."

They headed for the car with lightness in their steps, the air between them playful and affectionate. As they pulled out onto the gravel road, the sun was just beginning to dip low, painting the tops of the trees gold.

James reached for her hand. "Thanks for suggesting this. Just... All of it."

She squeezed his fingers. "Thanks for saying yes."

And for a little while longer, as the miles rolled by and the town crept closer, the world felt as simple as it had the day they first fell in love.

The diner buzzed with quiet chatter and the clink of silverware on ceramic plates. They were seated in the same booth as before, nestled beneath a framed photo of the town's founding from 1904. James couldn't help but grin at the predictability of it all the red leather booths, the laminated menus sticky at the edges, the same elderly couple at the counter sharing a slice of pie.

Leena nudged him with her knee under the table. "I think the banana cream pie is calling your name."

"I think it's whispering all the right things," he said with a smirk.

They shared a laugh as the waitress a woman in her late sixties with perfectly coiffed gray hair and a name-tag that read Janet came over to take their order. She had the kind of presence that made you feel like you were already family.

After placing their orders, James leaned back, his fingers drumming lightly against the edge of the table. "Hey, I never told you," he said casually, "when I went out for air earlier, I found something in the woods. An old cabin."

Leena raised an eyebrow. "A cabin?"

"Yeah, tucked away pretty deep. It looked... old. Like no one had been there in years. I left markers so I could find it again."

From across the room, Janet slowed her step as she passed with a coffee pot. Her ears had clearly picked up on the word.

"The old Wren's Hollow place?" She asked, turning toward them with interest.

James and Leena exchanged a glance. "I don't know what it's called," James said. "It's got a stone chimney, half-covered in ivy. Looks like it was built a hundred years ago."

Janet's eyes narrowed thoughtfully. "Yeah... that's Wren's Hollow. Folks around here don't go near it much these days. Wasn't always that way, though. That land has stories."

Leena leaned forward, intrigued. "What kind of stories?"

Janet poured them both fresh coffee before settling the pot back on her tray. "Oh you know, just stories people like to tell,"

James's brow furrowed. "Do you know who owns it now?"

"I don't think anyone," Janet said with a shrug. "It's county land now. Just sits there. Quiet. Like it's waiting. Some say it's cursed. Others say it's blessed."

Leena smiled softly. "Maybe it's just forgotten."

Janet tilted her head and gave a half-smile. "Funny thing about places like that. They don't stay forgotten forever."

The waitress moved on, leaving behind more than just coffee a sense of mystery, of history stirring beneath the surface.

James looked back at Leena, his mind already dancing with possibilities. Her eyes met his and something unspoken passed between them.

They were definitely going back.

As their meals arrived grilled cheese with tomato soup for her, and a burger piled high with onions and pickles for him they eased back into their booth, the world outside the diner fading to the edges. The golden hour glow filtered in through dusty blinds, and for a moment, it felt like they were characters in an old movie, the kind that ends with a kiss under string lights.

James reached across the table, brushing a crumb from the corner of Leena's mouth. "You know, this place kind of reminds me of the life we always said we wanted. Simple. Quiet. A little weird."

She smiled. "With pie. Lots of pie."

"And apparently, haunted cabins in the woods."

She nudged his foot beneath the table. "Haunted? You didn't mention haunted."

"Not haunted historical. Mysterious. Full of character."

"Mmm. That's what people say right before they get possessed."

They laughed, and just behind them, Janet returned with the check and another round of coffee refills. But she lingered again.

"You two planning to poke around Wren's Hollow tomorrow?" She asked, eyes gleaming like she already knew the answer.

James gave a half-shrug. "Might be. I marked the trail. Just... something about it stuck with me."

Janet nodded slowly, wiping her hands on her apron. "It tends to do that."

Janet lingered a moment longer, eyes drifting to the window as if the stories she held had their own weight. "There was a couple, back in the forties," she began, her voice softening with the edges of old memory. "He was some rich guy from back East, newly wedded. They say the two of them were so in love, just being near them gave off this aura. You could feel it. Like stepping into a sunrise."

Leena leaned in, caught in the story.

"One morning, he went out for a hike," Janet continued. "Never came back. They searched for weeks. Nothing. No tracks, no sign. Some folks say he slipped, maybe fell into a ravine or hit his head somewhere off-trail. Others think maybe he just vanished. Just left the world behind. But she... She waited. And waited. Wouldn't leave that place. Kept the lantern lit every night."

James's fingers stilled around his coffee cup.

"Eventually, the cabin was swallowed by the forest again. Time pulled it into the trees. Then in the seventies, another couple bought the land where you two are staying now. Built that cabin you're in to be a retreat a place to get lost for a bit. Thing is, no mention of Wren's Hollow was ever in the paperwork. Like the forest had covered it not just in trees, but in silence."

She wiped her hands on her apron again. "Folks say they still see her sometimes, Wren's bride. Out there in the mist, just wandering the woods. Still waiting. Still looking for the man who never came home."

Janet glanced between them. "Some people say it's a ghost story. Others say it's just a woman who loved too hard to forget."

James swallowed hard. Leena's hand found his again across the table. Neither of them spoke.

"If you do go," Janet added gently, "go together. The forest doesn't give up its secrets easy.
Leena tilted her head. "What happened to the woman who waited? The one you mentioned?"

Janet's smile thinned a little. "They say she kept the lantern in the window lit every night, even as the years passed. Eventually, she just stopped coming into town. But every now and then, someone swears they see that light flicker through the trees. And when it does... Something always stirs."

The booth went quiet.

"Sounds like the start of a ghost story," James said, trying to shake off the chill.

"Or maybe just the middle of a love story," Janet said softly.

She turned away and disappeared into the kitchen, leaving behind a silence that felt heavier than before.

Leena reached across the table, resting her hand over his. "I still want to see it. Tomorrow?"

He nodded. "Tomorrow."

Outside, twilight had fallen, but inside the diner, time seemed to bend and soften. And as they left, hand in hand, the door jingled shut behind them like the closing of a chapter one neither of them realized they'd needed so badly.

The air outside had cooled, the crisp breath of the coming night brushing past their skin as they stepped into the street. Neither said much for a few minutes both were lost in thought, still chewing on Janet's tale, still feeling the ghostly threads of a story that had lived far longer than either of them had walked this earth.

Leena gave James a sidelong glance. "You think there's any truth to it?"

He took a deep breath, his hand tightening slightly in hers. "I don't know. But the way she told it… I kind of hope there is."

"Even the sad parts?"

"Even those," he said, quiet. "Because she waited. Even when no one else believed. That kind of love it's rare."

They walked in silence for a bit longer, their footsteps echoing softly on the pavement.

Behind them, the light in the diner flickered once just once and then stayed lit. Like a whisper on the edge of night, not quite a memory, not yet a dream.

The car ride back was wrapped in the softness of twilight, head-lights carving golden beams through the trees as they wound their way home. Inside the car, the atmosphere was lightened by jokes meant to keep the eerie tone of Janet's tale at bay.

"So," James said with mock seriousness, "if we see a woman in white glowing in the woods, we floor it, right?"

Leena snorted. "Floor it? You'd be the first one out there trying to ask her what kind of lantern oil she uses."

"For science," he said, nodding. "Historical preservation."

She laughed, then rested her hand over his on the gearshift. "I like this us."

He looked at her from the corner of his eye, a warmth blooming in his chest. "Me too."

Back at their cabin, the shadows stretched long but didn't feel ominous. Instead, the woods whispered around them with the hush of evening settling in. They unloaded slowly, wine and leftovers tucked under arms, their steps unhurried. Inside, the space felt familiar now home, in a way neither of them had expected.

Leena set the wine on the counter and turned toward him. "Dance with me?"

He grinned. "No music?"

She shrugged. "We'll make our own."

They swayed in the dim light of the cabin's kitchen, arms wrapping around each other in a rhythm all their own. No choreography, no performance just two souls rediscovering a cadence they'd lost but never forgotten.

Their lips found each other again. Soft and knowing.

Later, curled together in the loft bed, the windows fogged with breath and warmth, Leena pressed her cheek to James's chest. "I missed this so much," she murmured.

He kissed the top of her head. "I missed you."

They slept, wrapped in each other, the kind that comes only after forgiveness has started to find its place.

In the pale morning light, James stirred first. He reached out, but the bed beside him was empty. Panic flickered in his chest for just a moment until the scent of coffee met his nose.

He sat up, running a hand through his hair, and smiled.

Outside the cabin, he found her on the porch, bundled in a blanket, coffee mug in hand.

He walked barefoot across the wood, sitting beside her without a word. For a time, they just watched the lake, still and shimmering beneath the lifting mist.

Eventually, he leaned close. "You started without me."

She smirked, not looking away the treeline. "You can catch up."

And as the forest stirred around them and the lake held its breath, it was clear: whatever today held, they'd face it together.

Back in the cabin, sunlight poured through the windows like a silent blessing. The scent of fresh pine wafted in with the morning breeze as James and Leena stepped into the warmth of their temporary sanctuary. Their hands remained entwined as they moved to the kitchen, laughter following them like a familiar echo.

"Pancakes again?" James asked with a crooked grin.

"Don't fix what isn't broken," Leena replied, already reaching for the flour.

They moved in tandem he got the eggs, she measured the batter. It was a dance of rediscovered rhythm, a quiet collaboration layered with easy smiles and fleeting touches. They joked about her overly precise measurements and his tendency to forget to flip the pancakes before they burned.

As breakfast sizzled on the skillet, their minds wandered to the day ahead.

"You still want to go to the cabin?" She asked gently.

James looked up from the coffee pot, nodding. "Yeah. I want you to see it. I want us to see it together."

"Okay," she said, giving a small nod. "Let's eat, pack a few things, and head out before it gets too late."

They set the table, sat down with their warm breakfast, and began to talk through what they'd need for the hike flashlights, water, a small first aid kit, just in case. Leena packed a notebook and charcoal pencils too, in case inspiration struck. James gathered the trail markers again this time adding a small hatchet and a length of orange ribbon to reinforce their path.

When the plates were cleared and bags were packed, they stood at the edge of the woods once more, the trail ahead familiar but still humming with mystery. Their eyes met, and with a deep breath, they stepped forward, ready for what the forest had hidden for so long.

Chapter 10

The trees rose tall and hushed around them as James and Leena stepped once more onto the winding trail. Their boots crunched over damp leaves, and their hands remained linked, even as the air turned cooler beneath the canopy.

This time, they came prepared. Backpacks slung over shoulders held bottled water, snacks, a flashlight. James had tied lengths of orange ribbon to the straps of his bag, already planning to reinforce the markers he'd made the day before. A small hatchet swung from his hip.

They didn't speak much at first. The forest had a way of silencing you without effort. Every now and then, Leena would glance upward, watching the way sunlight filtered through shifting branches. James, meanwhile, kept his eyes ahead, following the stone cairns and stick arrows he'd made, reinforcing them when needed.

After about half an hour, the trail narrowed into a ridge that overlooked a shallow ravine. The air smelled of moss and bark, and something older still something that felt like memory. James stopped and pointed to one of the markers. "See? Still here."

Leena gave a small nod, pulling out her phone again to check for signal. Nothing. Just the pale bar of a battery icon.

"I guess it's just us out here," she said, sliding the phone back into her pocket.

"I'll take that over a dozen calls any day," James replied.

They shared a quiet smile and kept walking.

At one point, they crossed an old stream-bed, now mostly dry. James reinforced a trail marker by stacking stones into a narrow column, then tied a ribbon to a nearby branch. Leena took a quick sketch of the shape of the land, just in case.

Eventually, the trees thinned. James slowed, gestured ahead.

"There," he said.

Through the veil of trees and brambles, the cabin appeared.

It looked almost exactly as it had the day before: stone chimney blackened with age, ivy curled along the roof line like a sleeping serpent. The door hung slightly ajar. No sign of movement. The place seemed to hold its breath.

Leena stepped forward slowly, eyes scanning the facade. She said nothing, only moved closer, her hand brushing James's.

They stopped just outside the door.

James looked over at her. "Ready?"

She nodded.

He pushed the door open.

The air inside was cool and still, thick with the scent of damp wood and must. Sunlight streamed through cracks in the roof, spotlighting motes of dust that drifted like ghosts. The floor creaked beneath their steps.

Leena looked around, fingers trailing along a broken bookshelf filled with rotted spines. A cobweb stretched like lace across the hearth. She turned slowly, absorbing the weight of forgotten years.

"It's beautiful," she whispered.

James moved carefully through the room. There were newer signs here too remnants of hikers or maybe folks who' had sought shelter from a storm. A rusted lantern, a torn rain poncho draped over a hook. A chipped thermos sitting upright on the mantle as if waiting for its owner to return.

He noticed a tattered pack tucked beneath a table, its contents spilled out long ago crushed granola bar wrappers, an old flashlight with corroded batteries, and beneath it all, a leather-bound journal weathered with age.

James picked it up gently, thumbing through the pages. Some were illegible from moisture damage, others still readable, each ink line trembling with someone's old thoughts.

Leena leaned in to read beside him. A page fluttered open:

"Spent three nights here. Something about this place makes you feel like you're standing on the edge of something sacred... or haunted. Maybe both."

Neither of them said a word. The air seemed heavier, not ominous but reverent, as if even the walls were listening.

Leena set her pack down, pulled out her sketchbook, and turned to a fresh page. Slowly, carefully, she began to draw. A woman wrapped in mist, standing at the edge of the trees, eyes searching some far-off place. Waiting. Hoping. A lantern glowing faintly beside her.

James left her to it, wandering deeper into the cabin. He found a shelf of old books most moldy or torn, but one or two salvage-able. Titles worn, spines cracked. A volume on native plants of the region. Another detailing folktales from early settlers. As he opened them, pages released that distinct smell of time, of dust, of pulp, of things long kept.

He flipped through a few stories, one short passage even spoke of a place in the woods where time folded inward, where people claimed to see those they'd lost.

James sat on an old stool, the book heavy in his hands. It wasn't just a story anymore. This place it wanted to be remembered. It had chosen to show itself.

Maybe, it had something to give back.

Across the room, Leena added the finishing strokes to her drawing, then paused, staring at the figure she'd conjured. Her heart was pounding, her throat tight. It wasn't just the woman she'd drawn it was herself, in another form. Waiting. Longing. Still holding the light.

James, distracted in his own thoughts, walked back across the creaking floorboards to where she sat. As he moved, one of the aged planks gave way beneath him with a sudden crack. His foot plunged through up to the shin, the jagged wood scraping against his leg.

"Shit!" He hissed, wincing as he pulled himself free. Leena rushed over, already reaching for the first aid kit.

"Are you okay?"

"Yeah," he grumbled, brushing dirt from his jeans. "Just my pride. And maybe a few splinters."

As he knelt to examine the break in the floor, something caught his eye beneath the splintered board a corner of leather, dusty but intact.

He reached down and tugged it free.

It was another journal. Small. The leather was dark red and embossed with delicate swirling patterns. He opened it, carefully flipping through pages filled with elegant, looping handwriting.

Leena leaned in. "It looks older."

The first page read:

"Our wedding day. I've never seen him smile like that. We are here, in the forest, and I think this will hold all the best parts of our beginning."

They shared a look.

The journal chronicled a love that had burned bright in the wilderness. The entries were short, but vivid. Notes about early mornings watching the mist rise over the treetops. Long afternoons spent cooking together, reading aloud, touching fingers across pages.

Later entries turned heavier.

"He's gone for a hike. I teased him for forgetting the compass, but he laughed it off. That laugh... It's the only thing keeping me calm now."

"Three days. No word. No sound. I light the lantern every night. I leave the door open. I wait. I wait."

They didn't read further. They couldn't. The words hit too close, echoing pain they both knew intimately.

James gently closed the journal and held it close. They sat in silence, the broken floor behind them, the cabin pressing in with stories aching to be heard.

Outside, the wind shifted through the trees.

They took one last look around the old cabin, tucking some books and the red journal safely into James's pack. As the daylight began to slip into amber tones, they retraced their steps through the quiet woods. The hike back felt shorter, though their legs were heavy with the weight of discovery and the deep, unspoken emotions stirred by the bride's journal.

When they stepped through the door of their own cabin, the scent of the place familiar now welcomed them like an embrace. Leena dropped her pack by the door with a sigh of relief and headed for the kitchen. James followed, rubbing his still-sore leg.

"Let's make something to eat before my foot falls off," he joked, shooting her a crooked smile.

She chuckled, already pulling ingredients from the pantry. "I should be the one limping emotionally wounded from hearing that crash."

Together, they moved through the kitchen something that hadn't existed just a week ago. Chopping vegetables, stealing bites, bumping hips in the narrow space. It wasn't about the food it was about the what they were finding again. About laughing together.

By the time dinner was plated and the rain returned to whisper against the windows, they sat cross-legged on the floor in front of the fireplace, sharing bites and stories, warmed from the inside out.

Later, they curled up on the couch, The the books resting between them. James grabbed the folklore book, while Leena returned to the bride's entries.

They read slowly, trading lines back and forth. The bride's handwriting grew shakier as the pages passed, but her words remained rooted in love. Unyielding hope. Each passage felt less like history and more like a prophecy.

At one point, Leena set the journal down, her gaze distant. "Do you think she ever stopped waiting?"

James shook his head gently. "No. I think... I think she became part of this place. Like the trees. Like the wind."

She nodded slowly, then leaned her head against his shoulder. He draped an arm around her and pulled her close, both of them silent, the fire crackling low.

It wasn't the end of the story. Not for them. Not yet. But as they sat there, with old ink and fading paper spread between them, something deeper rooted itself in their hearts.

They were still healing, still finding their way but whatever came next, they'd carry these stories with them.

Chapter 11

James stirred before dawn, the soft patter of rain whispering against the cabin roof like nature's lullaby. He blinked against the dimness, disentangling himself from the warm blankets without waking Leena. She lay curled on her side, one hand loosely tucked beneath her cheek, the faintest smile resting on her lips.

Quietly, James went into the kitchen. The air was cool, tinged with the scent of damp pine and the earthy perfume of last night's dying fire. He flicked on the stove top, dropped bacon into a pan, and cracked eggs into a bowl, whisking them slowly. As the bacon sizzled and the coffee pot gurgled to life, he leaned on the counter, glancing out the window where mist clung to the treetops.

He plated the food and poured two mugs of coffee, one with more cream, just the way she liked it. Carrying the tray with careful balance, he nudged open the bedroom door with his foot. Leena stirred as the aroma reached her.

"Mmm... am I dreaming?" she murmured, eyes fluttering open.

"Only if the dream includes scrambled eggs and bacon and perfectly brewed coffee."

She sat up, tousled and beautiful, reaching for the mug. "You spoil me."

"I plan to continue doing so until you make me stop."

They sat together on the bed, knees touching, sharing breakfast while rain tapped rhythmically on the windows. The world felt hushed, as if nature itself had taken a breath and was holding it just for them.

After they finished eating, Leena carried the dishes to the kitchen, but James waved her off and began washing them. She wandered back into the living room, drawn once more to the bride's journal resting on the coffee table.

Settling into the couch with a blanket around her shoulders, she opened the book and returned to the early pages entries filled with joy, awe, and a kind of tremulous hope. The bride had written of their wedding night, of laughter echoing off the trees, of the first time she called the cabin home.

"We danced in the kitchen to no music. We shared a bottle of wine and built a fire that smoked for hours because neither of us knew what we were doing. I've never been so happy."

Leena felt her throat tighten. These weren't just memories; they were reflections shadows of her own past with James. Every phrase mirrored her feelings from the early days, when everything felt fragile and magical and full of possibility. She read slowly, lips parted, heartbeat echoing with recognition.

Meanwhile, James pulled on a jacket and ducked out to the shed behind the cabin to gather more firewood. The rain had lessened to a soft drizzle, and the air smelled sharp. He took his time, stacking logs in his arms and breathing deeply. There was peace here. Healing.

When he returned, he saw her sitting in the same spot, the journal open in her lap, one hand resting on the page like it might drift away. Her eyes lifted to him, glassy but calm.

"You okay?" he asked gently.

She nodded. "It's strange. Like... like these are my words. Our words. Just dressed differently."

He set the firewood near the hearth and knelt beside her. She turned the book slightly so he could read with her.

"He makes me laugh when I forget how. He kisses my forehead when I pretend I'm not sad. He holds my hand like it's the first time, every time."

James exhaled slowly, the words sinking into him. "It's like we were always meant to find this."

Leena closed the book, laying it gently on the table. "Or it found us."

They sat in silence for a while, the fire crackling again, rain softening into mist.

She stood then, stretching the stiffness from her shoulders. "I should whip something up for lunch," she said with a soft smile.

As she moved into the kitchen, James wandered out to the dock. The rain had stopped completely, leaving behind a sheen of silver on the wooden planks and ripples in the lake that mirrored the clouds above.

He sat cross-legged near the edge,

James and just stared out across the water.
Back in the cabin, Leena stirred a pan on the stove top. The rich scent of warming butter filled the air. She moved around the kitchen with purpose, barefoot on the hardwood floor, the hem of one of James's flannel shirts brushing her knees.

As she reached for a plate, the record player in the corner clicked softly and began to spin. Without warning, the familiar scratchy opening of that old song began to play again slow, lilting, full of memory.

She froze for a moment, heart jumping, and then she just smiled to herself.
James heard the tune carry across the lake in the quiet. He stood slowly, closing the journal and cradling it in his arm, heading back toward the cabin. As he walked up the steps, the music swirled around him like a promise remembered.

Lunch was nearly ready.

And everything the journal, the laughter, the quiet stirrings of love remembered felt suspended in a kind of peace that neither of them had felt in years. It was as if the world had paused to let them simply exist in each other's presence, without expectation or noise.

James entered the cabin just as Leena was getting the last of the pasta. They exchanged a look that needed no words soft, adoring, full of healing. The record continued to hum behind them, and the air carried the smell of homemade sauce.

They sat down at the small kitchen table. As they ate, they traded little glances and warm, teasing smiles. There was no need to fill the silence, because even the quiet had become their language. Occasionally, Leena reached across the table to brush her fingers over his wrist or James would push her hair behind her ear with a gentle grin.

After the plates were cleared, James offered to do the dishes again. Leena dried while he washed, and somewhere in the middle of the simplicity of the moment, their hands met under the running water. They paused. Not from awkwardness but because they both felt it. That shift, the recognition. That feeling of home.

Outside, the mist had begun to rise from the lake, curling up like smoke. In the woods, the trees swayed slightly in the breeze, as though whispering their approval.

Back inside, two heart stitched a little closer.

They both decided with quiet agreement and curious wonder, to hike back to the old cabin once more. There was something sacred in that place. Something unfinished, perhaps. Or maybe something waiting.

They packed lightly just enough water and the journal. The forest was still slick with morning rain, the sun straining to peek through thick canopies overhead. Leaves shimmered with dew, the ground soft beneath their boots.

Their pace was unhurried. Conversation drifted between them like threads weaving a new tapestry. Other times, they were silent, the quiet between them full of understanding.

As they reached the trail marker James had built earlier carefully stacked stones and a few weathered branches they exchanged a look that needed no words. This place knew them. And they knew it too.

The path to Wren's Hollow felt different this time. Not lighter, necessarily, but familiar. Like visiting an old friend. This time, James and Leena held hands more deliberately, their fingers laced, the space between their steps closed.

When they reached the clearing, the cabin stood exactly as it had before weathered but dignified, steeped in time and untouched by modern life. Sunlight filtered down in soft shafts, catching on the mossy shingles and dancing through the tall grasses surrounding the porch.

James approached the threshold, eyes drawn again to the rough planks where the cabin tried to eat him. He stepped around it carefully, guiding Leena by the hand. She squeezed his fingers, grounding him.

Inside, the scent of old wood. Dust swirled in the air, dancing like tiny spirits caught in the stillness.

James wandered toward the shelves again, running his fingers over the old books, touching spines softened by time. Leena stepped toward the chair by the window and opened her sketchbook, starting a new drawing of the bride standing among the trees, her face tilted in quiet hope.

Neither of them spoke for a while. They didn't need to. Everything they felt pulsed in the silence the ache, the beauty and restoration.

It wasn't about finding answers. It never had been.

Chapter 12

Fall, 1944

The morning air was cool, crisp with the lingering scent of pine and woodsmoke, but the discomfort in Eva's abdomen pulled her from sleep before the light had fully crept through the windows of the small, rustic cabin nestled deep in the trees. It wasn't sharp just a low, dull ache that throbbed quietly, almost like her body whispering for her attention.

She shifted under the quilt, trying not to disturb the peace of the morning, but Wren stirred beside her anyway. His instincts had always been finely tuned, especially when it came to her.

"Eva?" His voice was gravel and warmth, the grogginess of sleep still clinging to it. He rolled toward her, eyes barely open, but his hand already found hers beneath the covers.

She forced a soft smile, her fingers squeezing his. "I think I slept wrong or something. Just a little sore."

His brow furrowed. He was always protective, perhaps more than he needed to be, but Eva never found it suffocating. It came from

The same place as his gentleness, the way he brewed her tea exactly how she liked it, or the way he read her poetry when storms rattled her nerves.

They had been married only a handful of months. The whirlwind of their romance still echoed around them in the quiet corners of the cabin. Wren born Warren Theodore Mason, but Eva had always called him Wren had returned from the war early, wounded but not broken. He never spoke much about the battlefield, only that it had changed him. Hardened him in some places, softened him in others.

After being sent home, he found himself restless in the quiet hills of eastern Kentucky, where his father had long suspected there was wealth buried deep beneath the forest floor. When coal was discovered black veins running thick through the hills it brought fortune quickly. And Wren, though modest, took his portion of that new legacy and disappeared into the trees.

He found Wrens Hollow the way someone might find a calling. The land felt ancient, sacred. He bought it outright, not for anything but to build. For her, for them. He spent months working beside the crew, laying the bones of the cabin, carving paths through the woods. He wanted to start their life somewhere untouched by the noise of the world.

Eva had met him in Louisville, a chance encounter during a spring rainstorm under the awning of a bookstore. She was buying paper and ink. He was looking for a first edition of Yeats. Their fingers brushed over the same door handle, and the rest, as they say, was fate.

They married three months later.

Now, in the hush of Wrens Hollow, they were trying to slow down. To be still. To learn what forever could look like.

Wren sat up and brushed her hair back from her forehead, his eyes scanning her face. "Sore how?"

"It's nothing, really. Just... A little discomfort. Probably slept weird," she murmured, leaning into his touch.

He didn't push. Just nodded, kissed her temple, and whispered, "Stay in bed. I'll make tea."

He was out of bed and moving through the cabin with a familiarity born of love. The floor creaked beneath his steps, and the fire popped softly in the hearth. Eva listened to the sounds of him moving about the clink of a kettle, the rustle of the tea tin and let her eyes close for a few more minutes.

Outside, the woods were painted in fire and gold. Autumn was full and heavy on the branches, and the light filtering through the trees was dappled and sleepy. Wrens Hollow felt like a place that had waited centuries for someone to notice it again.

Wren returned with two mugs, steam curling upward in lazy tendrils. He sat beside her, offering one.

"I added that honey you like. Thought it might help."

She accepted it, her fingers brushing his. "Thank you."

They sipped in silence for a while. She watched him over the rim of her mug. His face was still youthful, but the lines around his eyes spoke of things seen and endured. Still, there was peace in him now. He was hers. She was his.

Later, when the ache had dulled further, she dressed and joined him by the window, where he was reading from an old volume of Appalachian folklore. He had taken to collecting them books on local myths, herbal remedies, superstitions passed down through generations.

"You and your ghost stories," she teased lightly.

He smiled. "Just trying to learn what kind of magic lives in these woods."

She leaned against his shoulder, content.

No storm yet. Just the whisper of something stirring.

Eva rested her cheek against Wren's shoulder, letting the warmth of his body seep into her, anchoring her in that moment. The quiet between them wasn't empty it thrummed with something electric and unspoken, a resonance that neither time nor silence could dilute. Her eyes drifted beyond the glass, to the trees just beginning to shed their summer greens for richer, rust-colored gowns. Wrens Hollow was becoming a cathedral of fire and gold.

"You think the woods remember?" She asked softly, breaking the stillness.

Wren tilted his head, considering. "I think they never forgot."

Eva nodded, her fingers lightly curling over his forearm. "Feels like that sometimes. Like the trees are watching. Holding onto stories no one else wants to carry."

Wren chuckled gently, then tapped the book in his lap. "There's a legend in here about an old settler woman who vanished into the trees and came back speaking in tongues. Said the forest gave her visions."

Eva smiled, amused but curious. "What kind of visions?"

"She never said," he replied. "Only that she came back 'knowing how everything ends.'"

"That's comforting," she said dryly, and they both laughed an easy, real sound that cracked the hush like sunlight breaking through clouds.

She felt the ache again, a flicker in her lower abdomen, sharper this time, but she pressed it away. It wasn't the moment to worry. It was the moment to be here, with him, where it was warm and good and safe.

They spent the rest of the morning meandering through the cabin, tending to small chores they never quite finished. Wren chopped wood outside while Eva cleaned out the shelves she wanted to fill.

He wiped away dust with a damp cloth and rearranged jars of dried herbs and old buttons

By mid-afternoon, she had set up her easel near the back window where the sunlight hit just right. She hadn't painted in weeks. The move, the wedding, the travel everything had been so fast. But now, in the quiet lull of Wrens Hollow, her fingers itched for the brush again.

She dipped the tip into amber ocher and made her first slow stroke, watching it trail across the canvas like smoke. Wren, returning from outside, paused in the doorway and smiled when he saw her.

"Feels good, doesn't it?" he said.

She didn't look up, just nodded. "It does. Like remembering something I forgot I knew."

He crossed the room and kissed the top of her head. "Then paint it all. Everything this place gives you."

Eva felt the tenderness rise in her like a tide, and for a moment, she feared she'd cry. But she didn't. She dipped the brush again, pulled another line across the canvas, and felt her body settle.

Later that evening, they dined on roasted squash and wild mushrooms Wren had foraged earlier in the week. He had a knack for finding things in the woods more than once he'd brought home wild onions or ramps, proud as a child with a secret. They sat on the porch afterward, a blanket draped over their legs, sipping cider under a sky choked with stars.

Eva leaned her head on his shoulder, the ache in her belly still there but softened by his warmth. "Promise me," she whispered, "no matter what happens, no matter where we go, we'll always come back here."

Wren kissed her hair. "We built it with forever in mind."

The wind rustled through the trees like a hush across the lips of the forest. Somewhere in the distance, an owl called once, twice. The fire inside the hearth still crackled behind them, casting long shadows through the windows.

Throughout the night, the pain worsened. It deepened into something more persistent, a gnawing tension that woke Eva from restless dreams, her hands curled protectively over her lower belly. The warmth from the fire felt distant, the once-comforting crackle of the hearth now a sound far away from her growing anxiety. Her breath came in shallow bursts, beads of sweat blooming on her brow despite the cool of the cabin. She whimpered softly, gripping the quilt as a wave of nausea passed over her.

Alone in the dark, she turned her face toward the shadowed ceiling beams, trying to will the pain away, trying to be strong. Her thoughts wandered to their wedding day, the way Wren had looked at her with nothing but awe, to the smell of cedar in the cabin when they'd first arrived. She whispered his name once, not loud enough to call him, but as if speaking it might summon strength.

By morning, she was pale, her nightgown damp with sweat, and the ache had become sharp enough to steal her breath. Wren had dressed in a blur, his heart pounding with each second Eva gritted through another wave of pain. He kissed her forehead and promised he'd be back soon, his voice breaking against the lie.

The 120 roared to life, coughing in protest before settling into a

growl. Gravel sprayed out behind him as he sped down the unforgiving roads, twisting through the hills like a man running from
death.

He didn't notice the beauty of the autumn leaves or the chill in the
air. He barely felt the wheel in his hands. Every ounce of him was
focused on one thing: getting help.

Holes jarred his bones. Branches scraped at the sides of the car. Still
he pressed harder, white-knuckling the steering wheel. The path
to town was no simple journey it wound like a serpent through
the hills, unforgiving and narrow. He skidded around bends, heart
hammering louder than the engine.

All he saw was the image of Eva's face, pale and scared.

He drove like a man possessed, every instinct screaming to get help,
to bring back a doctor, to not let this place this sacred space they'd
built with dreams and laughter become a site of sorrow.

He left behind the love of his life, lying in the bed they had shared,
her fingers clinging to the edge of the quilt like it might anchor her.
Her breath was shallow, her eyes fixed on the door long after he was
gone, trusting he'd return with salvation.

 Alone again in the hushed cabin, the silence pressed in like the
weight of a second skin. The ache had grown into something sharp
and shifting, curling through her body in waves that stole her
breath.

Eva shifted with effort, the simple act of turning over stealing what
little strength she had left. She stared at the ceiling beams, tracing
their lines with unfocused eyes, her thoughts tumbling into fear.
What if he didn't make it in time?

What if she was losing something more than just control over her
own body? No hospital nearby. No midwife. No phone. Just trees,

endless trees, and the man she loved barreling down treacherous roads to find someone, anyone, who could help.

The pain was no longer something she could reason with it surged now, like a second heartbeat. Her hands trembled as she reached for the glass of water Wren had left on the nightstand. It tipped, spilling across the wood floor, soaking the edge of the rug. She cried out not from the mess, but from the sudden, jarring reminder of how fragile everything had become.

She clutched the pillow, pressing it against her abdomen, as if pressure could stop the tide. Her thoughts swam between prayers and memories: the way Wren had knelt in the dirt, covered in sawdust, asking her to move here; the way he held her hand at night, even in sleep; the way they'd danced barefoot on the porch to records, dreaming out loud about children and quiet holidays.

Her body tensed again. She whimpered. And as tears slipped silently down her cheeks, she whispered his name not loud enough for anyone to hear, but with the last thread of strength she could muster.

"Please, Wren. Hurry."

When he reached the doctor's office in town, he didn't even cut the engine. He leapt from the car, shouting before his feet hit the stoop.

"Doctor Moore! I need you now!"

The elderly man appeared in the doorway, eyes sharp behind his spectacles.

"She's hurting Eva she's in pain, bad," Wren panted.

Dr. Moore grabbed his bag without another word. As they climbed into the car, the doctor asked, "Why the hell didn't you bring her?"

Wren's hands tightened around the wheel. "The roads. The panic. The way she was feeling... I didn't think she'd make it. I didn't want to take the risk."

The doctor nodded grimly. "Then drive, son. And don't miss a turn.".

Chapter 13

Wren drove like a seasoned race driver, his knuckles bone-white against the wheel, the doctor gripping the dashboard beside him. The Packard skidded along curves and rumbled across uneven ground. They made the drive in less than half the time it had taken him before.

As they reached the cabin, the tires barely found purchase on the leaf-littered clearing. Wren was out of the car before it stopped, his boots slamming against the earth as he ran to the door, throwing it open with a crash.

"Eva!"

No answer.

His heart thudded in his ears as he rushed inside, the warmth of the fire still glowing low in the hearth, casting long shadows across the floor.

Then he saw her.

She was lying on the wooden floor just between the hearth and the kitchen, half-curled on her side, her nightgown stained a deep, dark red. Her face was pale, a shade of porcelain that shouldn't exist outside of statues. Her hair clung damply to her temples, and her breath came in faint, uneven gasps barely audible over the pounding in Wren's chest.

Blood.

It was everywhere. Pooled beneath her. Soaked into the wood. Streaked along the floor where she had tried to drag herself, maybe to the door, maybe to the table to sit, to wait for him.

Wren dropped to his knees beside her, his voice cracked and useless. "Eva... oh God, Eva."

Dr. Moore was already there, pulling back the blankets that had slipped from the couch and checking her pulse with fingers trained by years and sharpened by urgency. He opened his bag, pulled out cloth, scissors, morphine.

"She's lost a lot of blood," he muttered, mostly to himself. "Damn it. This should've been a hospital delivery."

Wren's face crumpled, anguish spreading like wildfire. "I didn't know. We didn't know."

"She was further along than you realized, or maybe something ruptured," the doctor said, shaking his head. "You weren't ready for this. No one was."

Eva stirred faintly, her fingers twitching, her lips parting as if to say his name. Her eyes blinked open for a moment, dazed and unfocused, catching his.

He gathered her gently, resting her head against his chest, whispering broken words he couldn't even hear himself. "I'm here. I'm here now. I'm so sorry."

She groaned softly, and a tear slipped from her eye, carving a silent trail down her cheek.

The doctor worked as best he could with what little he had pressure, stitching torn tissue, cleaning what he could. But this wasn't a hospital, and 1944 didn't offer much mercy for women in Eva's position.

When it was done, when her bleeding slowed and her breaths deepened slightly, Wren held her in the bed, her body weak and trembling, her fingers clutching his like a lifeline.

The cabin felt still again but not in peace. It was the stillness of aftermath. The air was thick with iron and sorrow, with everything unsaid. The silence screamed.

The fire cracked faintly, and outside, the wind rustled the trees like a hush being passed from limb to limb. Inside, a man held the love of his life and prayed she wouldn't drift away with the dawn.

The leaves were turning gold when Eva returned to the hollow. After several long days in the hospital days where her life hung in delicate balance, she was finally strong enough to make the journey back. But she returned changed. They both did.

The doctor had delivered the news with care and a lowered gaze. Eva would never be able to carry a child to term again. Something inside her, already fragile, had torn beyond repair.

Wren had nodded, silent, his jaw clenched. Eva had simply stared out the hospital window, watching the wind pull leaves from the trees as if nature itself was grieving with her.

But they didn't speak of despair not aloud. Not when they came home. Not in Wrens Hollow.

Instead, they lived as if hope were still something that could be shaped with their hands.

They laughed. They cooked together. They built shelves from pine planks and decorated the mantle with little treasures found on long walks twigs shaped like hearts, a bluebird's feather, river stones smoothed by time.

On the porch at night, Eva would press her head to Wren's shoulder, and he would kiss the top of her hair and hum a song they'd danced to at their wedding.

She'd begun writing again more than just notes in a journal. Full entries. Pages. Volumes. She wrote of their wedding day, of the way Wren's tie had been crooked and how he'd whispered a joke just before she said her vows. She wrote about the cabin, how it smelled like cedar and promise. About how Wren always cleared his throat before saying something important, how he folded his socks in exact pairs but never capped the ink on his pen. About how his hands were always warm.

She wrote of love. Not the kind found in poems, but the kind that survived.

Wren, too, found himself lighter in some strange way. He whittled in the mornings and read in the afternoons. He made her tea before she asked for it and left fresh wildflowers in a jar beside her notebooks.

There were quiet days and loud days. Days where Eva would go still for long stretches, her pen paused mid-page, staring at something only she could see. Wren never asked what she saw. He just brought her a blanket and kissed her cheek.

The hollow was still their dream even if the shape of that dream had changed. They were learning to hold it differently now, gentler, with more care. It was no longer about what they would build or who they might raise. It was about who they already were. What they had endured. And the way they still found one another, again and again, in the silence.

At night, when the forest whispered, they whispered back. Two voices. Still together.

Wren often thanked whatever instinct had led him to buy her the journal the one with the soft leather cover in her favorite shade of dusty plum. He remembered the day he saw it in the window of a tiny stationery shop in town, tucked between thick, bound ledgers and ink pots. Something about it had called to him, as if it already knew the hand that would hold it.

Eva had clutched it to her chest like a treasure when he gave it to her, her eyes soft and shining. And now, that little book had become more than just parchment and thread. It was a sanctuary, a place where she poured her thoughts when her voice faltered or when the weight of the day grew too much to speak aloud.

Besides painting, it was the one place she could go to sort the chaos in her heart. She filled its pages with fragments of memory, sketches of dreams, and recollections of Wren's laughter. Some pages were raw and trembling. Others carried a gentleness like feathers caught in wind. But each word was a step forward, a small reclaiming of peace.

And from that place of quiet healing, their days grew softer measured by shared meals, new stories, and the simple presence of one another. Wren often caught himself staring at her while she wrote, gratitude blooming in his chest like spring after the frost. The dream of Wrens Hollow hadn't withered with their loss. It had only changed shape becoming something more sacred.

They spent hours wandering through the trees, collecting moss-covered stones and tracing deer tracks in the soil. Wren fixed the creaky porch swing while Eva painted the light filtering through the trees. They didn't speak much of what had happened, but the silence between them felt honest, not heavy.

It was during one of those walks early October, the forest glowing gold and copper when Wren paused at the ridge overlooking the bend in the stream. He turned to her with a wistful half-smile and said he needed to see more of the land, feel it under his boots. Just a short hike, he promised. To the western ridge and back. He wanted to map out the edges of the property, maybe mark where he'd build a small studio for her painting come spring.

Eva had laughed, teasing him about remembering the compass this time, brushed the hair from his eyes, and reminded him not to be gone long. He kissed her forehead, tucked the journal she'd been writing in close to her side, and vanished into the rustling hush of the woods.

Chapter 14

Leena sat curled on the edge of the couch back in their cabin, the journal open in her lap, a throw blanket wrapped tightly around her legs. Rain tapped gently against the windows, a sound that mirrored the steady, disbelieving thud of her heart as she read through Eva's account of the miscarriage the pain, the helplessness, the quiet horror of realizing the dream they'd nurtured had slipped away. The words blurred as tears filled her eyes. Each sentence felt like a whisper from another time, one that had somehow lived in her chest all along.

James was in the small kitchen, slicing vegetables and humming quietly to himself, unaware of the storm building behind her eyes. She turned another page and read about the hospital stay, the sterile halls, the kindness in the nurse's touch, the doctor's hesitant words 'never again.' The crushing finality of it hit Leena like a wave. Her fingers trembled.

Eva had written about the studio Wren wanted to build for her, the way he kept the dream alive even as theirs had been altered forever. That thread of hope that fierce, stubborn hope wound itself around Leena's heart like a lifeline.

She shut the journal slowly and stared into the fire. Something in her had shifted. They hadn't talked about it not really. Not the miscarriage. Not the unraveling that had come afterward. The silence had kept them distant, floating parallel in the same grief. But now...

She glanced toward James. He caught her eye and smiled, still unaware of the journal's weight. The warmth in his smile twisted something inside her.

Maybe tonight, she thought. Maybe after dinner. Maybe it's finally time to say the words out loud.

She stood, folding the blanket with care, letting the journal rest gently atop it. She walked toward the kitchen, her heartbeat heavy, her mouth dry, but her resolve steady.

Dinner was almost ready. The kitchen carried the warm scent of roasted vegetables, the sizzle of oil a subtle accompaniment to the nervous energy beginning to simmer in her chest. She leaned against the doorway, watching him move methodical, calm, the sleeves of his shirt rolled to the elbows as he focused on the skillet in front of him.

He hadn't noticed the redness around her eyes, or the way she clutched her hands tightly in front of her. But she wasn't ready to speak just yet.

They ate at the small table near the fireplace, soft lamplight casting their shadows across the walls. They made idle conversation about the storm, about the firewood, about maybe checking out the eastern ridge the next day.

But Leena's mind wasn't there.

It was with Eva. With the pain in that cabin decades ago. With the ache of love stretched thin by loss.

As James stood to clear the plates, she stopped him with a touch to his hand.

"Can we talk?" she asked.

He turned slowly, reading something deeper in her eyes, and nodded. He sat back down.

Leena drew in a breath that seemed to reach the bottom of her lungs. "I never blamed you, you know. Not really. For what happened."

James blinked, startled. "Leena "

"Let me finish," she said gently. "It hurt. It still does. And I shut you out. I know I did. I felt broken and empty and like I wasn't allowed to grieve because... I didn't even know how. I didn't want to be touched, and then I was angry that you didn't touch me. I pushed, and you... you drifted."

He reached for her hand, and she let him. His grip was warm, grounding.

"You weren't the only one drifting," he said. "I should've fought harder. But every time I tried to reach you, you were so far away. And I didn't know how to bring you back."

She swallowed. "Reading her words… Eva's… it's like she was telling our story. The loss. The distance. But she kept writing. She kept finding a way to speak it."

They sat in silence, fingers intertwined, the fire crackling softly nearby.

"I want us to be like them," she whispered. "Still in love. Still trying. Even if it hurts. Especially because it hurts."

James nodded, his eyes glassy with tears he wasn't ashamed to let fall. "Then let's do it. All of it. The truth, the mess, the healing. Together."

Outside, the rain eased into a hush. Inside, something unspoken finally took root.

Not a second chance, more like a continuation.

They sat in the hush of the firelight, no longer fighting the weight of the past, but learning to carry it together. And as the flames danced in the hearth, so too did a fragile sense of grace threaded with sorrow, yes, but also with the promise of something unbroken rising in its place.

The conversation continued deep into the evening. Quiet. Honest. And beautifully overdue. Their conversation teetered on love, with a hint of disdain the wounds were still very much real. But they were on their way to salvation, sitting and talking as the fire died down.

A single beep came from her cellphone on the counter top. No message. No notification. Battery half full.

Just a beep.

It caught them both off guard.

James looked over at the phone, brows furrowed. "Did you get service?"

Leena stood slowly, crossing to the counter and picking it up. She checked the screen. "Nothing. Just... a beep."

They exchanged a glance, unease threading the air between them. The fire crackled one last time, then settled into embers.

James let out a slow breath. "Maybe just a glitch."

Leena didn't answer. She was still staring at the phone, her fingers curled around it a little too tight. Outside, the wind sighed against the windows, and deep in the forest, something unseen stirred.

As the fire dwindled into a gentle glow, they had sat close on the couch, not needing to fill the silence with words. The soft hush of the flames and the steady rhythm of their breathing were enough. Eventually, the heat between them shifted subtle, then urgent. What began as a kiss beneath the blanket turned into something that felt almost holy.

They moved to the bedroom with the reverence of old lovers re-discovering each other, touching like it might be the last time, like every second was a question answered. They undressed each other slowly, deliberately layers peeled away with gentleness and fire alike. It wasn't just lust. It was something else. A kind of making that had nothing to do with bodies and everything to do with forgiveness, with choosing each other all over again.

When they finally fell asleep, wrapped in the heat of that moment, it was with hearts unburdened and breathing synced like lullabies.

James woke slowly, his body tangled in warm sheets, the cabin dim with the hush of early morning light. The smell of coffee was the first thing that tugged him out of sleep a rich, grounding scent that drifted from the kitchen and settled like a memory across the wooden beams. For a moment, he smiled, half-asleep, imagining Leena standing barefoot at the counter,
He turned over, the space beside him was empty.

He sat up, blinking the sleep from his eyes. The quiet was too com-plete. No clinking of mugs or soft footsteps across creaky floor-boards. Just the distant hush of wind across the lake.

Throwing on a sweater, James walked across the room, the cabin warm from the embers still glowing in the hearth. He followed the scent of coffee to the kitchen where a full mug sat untouched on the table. Still warm. But no sign of Leena.

He stepped outside.

The world was blanketed in a gentle mist, soft and silver, curling around the pines and across the surface of the lake. There, at the end of the dock, sat Leena. Wrapped in a thick cardigan, her legs tucked beneath her, the journal resting open in her lap. She didn't look up as he approached, her eyes scanning the page with a quiet intensity that told him she was somewhere else entirely.

He walked softly down the dock, the wood cool beneath his feet, until he reached her side. Leena glanced up, offering him a faint, tired smile before returning her gaze to the page.

"Coffee's inside," she murmured, her voice distant, as if she hadn't quite come back to this moment yet.

James sank down beside her, following her eyes to the journal. Eva's handwriting danced across the page, elegant and looping, full of longing and something deeper an ache that stretched far beyond the ink.

"I watch the trees and wonder if they've seen him, if the wind carries his voice back to me. Each day I wait, and each night I dream of his return. The silence grows thicker. He said he'd only be gone a few hours."

Leena turned the page with careful fingers. Her voice was quiet. "She waited for him. Days. Weeks. Writing letters he'd never read."

James exhaled slowly, staring out at the lake. "She didn't know he wasn't coming back."

"She still doesn't," Leena said softly. "At least… not in here." She tapped the journal.

They sat like that for a long moment, the mist slowly thinning as the morning sun reached for them. It felt sacred, that silence not empty, but full. The kind that held memories too big for words.

James finally spoke. "You ever wonder what would've happened if we hadn't come here?"

Leena shut the journal and looked at him. "All the time. But then I remember I was already disappearing, even before we left. You were too."

He nodded. "This place pulled us back. Her story… maybe it's telling us how to keep going."

Leena leaned her head on his shoulder, her hand still holding the journal. "She kept writing like he'd walk back through the door any second. Maybe she thought if she just wrote it down, if she believed hard enough…"

James wrapped his arm around her, anchoring them both. "We'll finish the story. Not just hers. Ours too."

They sat on the dock until the sun was well above the trees, until the mist burned off and the world shimmered with light and promise. And still, she held the journal in her lap, as if it had become a part of her. A mirror to her grief. A map to something better. Later, as the sun climbed higher,

Leena finally closed the journal and rose to her feet, her legs stiff from sitting so long. She looked down at James and smiled softly. "Let's go for a walk," she said. "I need to stretch my legs"

James stood beside her, brushing off his hands. "Yeah, let's explore a little."

They followed the worn path that circled around the lake, their steps slow and unhurried. The air was fresh and cool, still holding the damp sweetness of early morning mist. Pine needles crunched beneath their boots, and the lake shimmered beside them, mirroring the sun's slow rise. The trail curved through the trees, past moss-covered rocks and the distant sound of water trickling over stone.

They talked about nothing and everything about the birdsong, the shape of clouds, the way the forest seemed to hum with its own kind of wisdom. There were long stretches of silence, this silence breathed between them, soft and open.

After a while, they returned to the cabin, cheeks flushed and hands warm from holding.

"I should make us something for lunch," Leena said, brushing a lock of hair from her face.

James nodded. "Sounds good. I'll sit out here a bit longer. I might read while you cook."

Back inside the cabin, Leena took her time putting the journal away, still absorbing the weight of its words. She glanced toward James, who remained seated on the dock, the light wind rustling his hair as he opened the book, The pages were faded, the ink slightly smudged in places from what looked like old water damage. But the words were still legible.

James sat quietly on the dock, the book resting open in his lap, the words of someone he'd never met echoing softly in his mind. The water lapped gently beneath him, rhythmic and soothing, yet he felt an unease he couldn't quite name.

Footsteps sounded softly behind him, and Leena's presence warmed the air even before she reached him. She lowered herself beside him, tucking her legs beneath her and leaning in to read over his shoulder.

"What did you find?" She asked quietly.

"Just some old folk tales about these woods."

Chapter 15

Leena took the book gently, scanning the lines quickly. Her brow furrowed. "They felt it too the pull, the sense of being watched.

James shook his head slowly, staring out at the lake. "I don't know. But it feels like we're part of something bigger now. Like these woods are holding onto stories that aren't finished yet."

A single, sharp beep echoed suddenly from inside the cabin, breaking the tranquility. Both turned, startled. Leena looked puzzled. "What was that?"

"The phone again," James said, his voice tight. "It keeps doing that, just random beeps. No messages or notifications."

Leena glanced toward the cabin, unease creeping into her features. "It's strange."

James sighed deeply, feeling tension knot between his shoulders. "Everything feels strange now. Like we're not entirely alone."

Leena leaned her head against his shoulder, letting out a slow breath. "Maybe that's why we're here to finish these stories. Or at least to try."

He wrapped an arm around her, the afternoon sun warming their faces even as a chill settled in his chest. Birds called softly from the trees, and a gentle breeze whispered secrets through the leaves. It felt peaceful and ominous at once a beautiful, fragile balance they both sensed could tip at any moment.

"Tomorrow," James finally said, voice quiet but steady, "we go back to the old cabin. We look deeper. We find whatever answers are waiting for us there."

Leena nodded against him, her eyes closed, trusting in him, in them. "Tomorrow," she echoed softly, "we'll face whatever it is together."

They sat for a long while, each lost in thoughts of past and present, each understanding that the threads they followed were weaving them ever tighter into a story much older than themselves. James's unease grew quietly, like shadows lengthening with the setting sun, as if the woods themselves were holding their breath, waiting for whatever came next.

Then, as the last glow of daylight receded into twilight, something flickered in the distance a faint, hesitant light among the trees.

James sat up sharply, heart quickening. "Leena," he whispered urgently, nudging her gently. "Do you see that?"

She followed his gaze, squinting into the gathering darkness. Her breath caught softly. "A light...out there. In the woods."

They watched in tense silence, the tiny flickering glow pulsing gently, beckoning them from the shadows.

Without another word, they stood, a silent decision passing between them. Leena's mind raced. Was it Eva? Was it just a figment of her imagination, stirred by hours spent reading about her? No, it couldn't be. James had seen it first.

Inside the cabin, they quickly gathered their flashlights, jackets, and a few essential items. They exchanged a glance resolute, united and stepped out into the encroaching darkness. The flickering light continued to pulse gently, a soft beacon guiding them deeper into the heart of the woods.

Branches brushed against them as they moved cautiously forward, the path uncertain beneath their feet. Shadows danced in the narrow beams of their flashlights, creating illusions of movement and whispering secrets in rustles of leaves. The light ahead pulsed rhythmically, almost hypnotic in its consistency, leading them on.

"Stay close," James murmured, gripping Leena's hand tighter.

"I am," she breathed, her eyes wide, fixed on the elusive glow. Her heart pounded, each step forward an act of trust against the unknown.
Minutes felt like hours, their progress slow and careful, until the dense trees finally parted slightly. Before them stood the silhouette of the old cabin, dark and solemn. The flickering light vanished abruptly, plunging them into sudden darkness, as if the woods had finally withdrawn their invitation, leaving them standing uncertainly in the wavering beams of their flashlights.

James swept his flashlight slowly around the clearing, shadows leaping and retreating in its path. "It's gone," he whispered, a note of confusion and frustration in his voice.

Leena sighed softly, her breath forming a brief cloud in the crisp night air. "Whatever it was, I think it wants us to wait."

James glanced at her, unease evident in the lines of his face. "I don't like this," he admitted quietly. "Let's head back for tonight."

She nodded in agreement, and together they turned away from the old cabin, retracing their steps carefully through the now seemingly thicker darkness. Despite their flashlights illuminating the path ahead, the silence felt heavier, more oppressive, as though something watched them retreating, unseen but ever-present.

The warmth of their own cabin welcomed them back, a stark contrast to the mysterious and unsettling woods they'd left behind.

Once inside, James secured the door firmly, casting a last wary look toward the forest before drawing the curtains closed.

They moved quietly to the couch by the fire, settling into its comforting warmth. James stared into the flickering flames, brow furrowed deeply. "What do you think it was?" he finally asked, his voice low and contemplative.

Leena shook her head gently, pulling a blanket tighter around her shoulders. "I don't know. Maybe a reflection, maybe something natural...but it felt like more. It felt intentional."

James rubbed his face tiredly, leaning back against the couch. "That's exactly what bothers me it felt like something or someone was trying to get our attention. Like it wants us to follow, or find something specific."

"Or someone," Leena murmured, her eyes distant, reflecting the dancing firelight. "Eva, Wren, whoever wrote those journals..."

James nodded slowly. "All of it feels connected. But connected to what? And why us?"

They sat quietly, the crackling fire filling the silence between them. Questions lingered in the air, unanswered but shared, as they tried to make sense of the strange and mysterious occurrences that had drawn them deeper into the heart of these woods.

Chapter 16

Leena awoke just before dawn, her eyes opening slowly to the soft, grayish light filtering through the curtains. The cabin was quiet except for the faint, comforting crackle of embers still glowing in the hearth. Despite the warmth beneath the covers, a chill crept over her skin, raising goosebumps. An uneasy feeling had settled deep within her chest, a subtle whisper of apprehension she couldn't quite shake.

She carefully slipped from the bed, wrapping herself in a thick sweater and walking quietly toward the kitchen. She glanced back at James, who slept soundly, his features softened in the tranquility of rest. She chose not to wake him just yet, needing a moment alone to process the turmoil stirring within her.

Leena prepared coffee mechanically, her thoughts drifting to the strange occurrences of the past few days. The journal entries, the mysterious lights, the haunting echoes of the woods, it was overwhelming yet strangely compelling. She sipped the hot coffee, the familiar bitterness grounding her in the present, giving her strength.

Stepping out into the early morning chill, Leena felt an immediate stillness, as though nature itself were holding its breath. The sky was transitioning from gray to muted shades of gold and rose, casting an ethereal glow across the landscape.

She navigated the trail with determination, her heart pounding softly in rhythm with her steps. The path was becoming familiar now, each tree and turn embedded in her memory. Still, her nerves tightened with each stride, the woods feeling alive and watchful.

As she approached the clearing where the old cabin stood, the rising sun illuminated it in soft relief, making the weathered structure appear both welcoming and foreboding. She paused at the edge of the clearing, drawing a slow, steadying breath.

"Eva," she whispered softly, almost as a greeting. The name hung gently in the morning air, an acknowledgment, a bridge between past and present.

Steeling herself, Leena moved forward, drawn toward the cabin door and whatever secrets lay beyond its threshold.

The door creaked open beneath her touch, its weathered hinges protesting softly. Inside, the air was cool and dense, heavy with memories long past. Shafts of sunlight pierced through gaps in the walls, casting fragmented patterns across the dusty floorboards. Leena stepped cautiously, her gaze sweeping over the room still furnished with the remnants of lives once lived here. A faded couch, an old wooden table, shelves lined with books coated in layers of dust.

She moved deeper into the cabin, her footsteps careful but resolute.

"Why are you calling me here, Eva?" She asked softly, her voice echoing faintly within the room. "What do you need me to see?"

Opening the journal, Leena found herself flipping to pages she hadn't fully absorbed yet, words Eva had written near the end of her entries. Her breath caught as she read:

"I see him in the shadows now, always at the edge of my vision, whispering words I can't understand. Is it madness or truth? Am I losing myself, or am I being found?"

The words sent chills racing down Leena's spine, her pulse quickening. Suddenly, the sharp, unmistakable beep of her cellphone echoed through the cabin, breaking the tense silence. Leena gasped softly, heart thundering against her ribs as she quickly silenced the phone, noting with confusion that there was no message or notification.

Shaken, Leena made her way toward a bedroom at the back of the cabin, stepping carefully across creaking floorboards. The room was sparse, the bed frame sagging under the weight of age, a worn chair resting in the corner. Her eyes immediately fell upon the rusted pool of blood, dark and ominous, staining the floorboards as though it had risen from deep within the wood itself.

Slowly, she sank onto the floor near the haunting stain, unable to tear her gaze away. A heaviness settled over her, the weight of grief and loss pressing upon her chest, echoing through time, connecting her inexplicably to Eva's sorrow.

Minutes passed, stretching into a timeless blur. Leena reached out, her fingers brushing the rough, stained wood. The chill of the room seemed to seep deeper into her bones, wrapping around her like a shroud. She closed her eyes briefly, trying to steady her racing heart, but vivid images of Eva's anguish flashed behind her eyelids.

Taking a deep breath, Leena opened her eyes again, determination flickering through the fear. She knew there was something crucial she was meant to find here, some message or truth buried beneath years of sorrow and solitude. Her gaze drifted upward, catching sight of something tucked behind a loose wooden panel in the wall beside the bed.

Carefully, Leena rose and approached the panel, her fingers trembling slightly as she pried it open. Hidden within the small recess was a bundle of faded letters tied with brittle twine. Her heart skipped a beat as she withdrew them, feeling a powerful surge of connection to the past. Holding them tightly, she returned to the floor, the letters resting gently in her lap as she prepared herself to uncover another layer of Eva's haunting story.

She untied the twine slowly, reverently, as though disturbing the slumber of ghosts. The first letter's script was graceful but unsteady, ink faded and edges worn. It wasn't just Eva's words that struck her but the vulnerability, the raw, untouched ache of someone left behind.

As Leena read the opening lines, the cabin seemed to exhale, as if finally relinquishing a secret long held close.

"My dearest Wren, today the pain returned not the kind that tears flesh the kind that pulls at the soul..."

Tears welled in Leena's eyes as she continued, feeling Eva's heartbreak thread through every word, each line a mirror to her own buried grief.

The next letter trembled slightly in her hands. "They said I'd never be a mother, but I still set a place at the table. I still dream of little feet running through these halls. I still imagine you lifting our child in your arms and laughing like you used to."

The images carved into her mind, Leena turned to another. "The wind speaks of you. I think the trees remember. Or maybe I've simply lost the boundary between memory and madness."

Another beep from her cellphone shattered the stillness, sharper this time, more urgent. Her hands froze. Again, no message.

She tucked the letters carefully back into their hiding place and stood. The air felt thicker now, the atmosphere saturated with emotion too long repressed. Leena backed out of the room, her thoughts swirling, her heart pounding.
Something was building, something Eva had tried desperately to say.

And Leena was beginning to hear it.

She stepped carefully back into the main room of the cabin, the light shifting through the cracks in the walls as morning advanced. Her breath was steady now, though her heart still beat with the echo of those words. She walked to the window and gazed out, unsure of what to do next. The trees swayed gently, whispering stories only the still could hear.

The answers were close. Closer than ever.

And Leena knew she wouldn't leave until she found them.

James stirred as the morning light crept into the bedroom. He blinked against the soft haze, the smell of coffee lingering faintly in the air, warm and grounding. But something was off.

The air inside the cabin felt... Different. Not quite cold, not quite warm more like a hush had settled into every corner, a silence that carried weight. He sat up slowly, stretching, only to realize the space beside him was empty. No Leena.

He glanced around the room. Her sweater was gone. The bed looked undisturbed, save for his half. Something deep in his chest tensed. Not worry yet but something near it. A thread pulled taut.

The coffee pot was still warm when he entered the kitchen, a half-drunk mug resting on the counter. Her scent lingered faintly in the air lavender, cedar, and something softer, unmistakably her.

He opened the front door, stepping out onto the porch. The morning mist clung to the trees like breath made visible, and the forest was as still as a held note. James stared into the trees, a low thrum of concern beginning to build.

She hadn't taken the car. No note. Just gone.

Something was stirring in the woods. And Leena was out there with it.

The thought sank like a stone in his chest. It wasn't just the woods that unnerved him. It was the heaviness of the air, the way the mist didn't move, how the birds had not yet dared to welcome the day. It felt... wrong.

He stepped down from the porch, gravel crunching beneath his boots as he scanned for any sign of where she might have gone. No footprints in the dirt, no trail disturbed. Just the distant echo of his own breath, and the rising panic threading through his veins.

"Leena?" He called, voice firm but not loud. It sounded strange out here too loud, yet swallowed too quickly.

No answer.

He went back inside, grabbed his coat, and checked the kitchen again. Her mug was still warm, barely a sip taken. She hadn't planned to be gone long. That's what he told himself, clinging to it like a rope.

But something didn't sit right.

He made his way back to the bedroom, trying not to let his imagination spiral. He noticed her sketchpad on the edge of the bed the one she kept beside her at night like a sacred artifact. It was open, the pages ruffled like they'd been hurried through. As he reached for it, a sharp, electronic beep pierced the silence.

James froze.

The sound came from Leena's phone but where was it

his heart skipped had she not taken it

The unease bloomed like smoke in his chest. That sound had happened before the same eerie beep, as if the phone was being used by something else entirely. He didn't believe in ghosts. But this place... It made you believe in possibilities you couldn't quite name.

"Where did you go?" he whispered, eyes lifting to the woods beyond the window.

James didn't hesitate any longer. He grabbed his flashlight, tucked a small hunting knife into his coat pocket just in case and made for the trail behind the cabin, the one that led toward Wren's Hollow.

Because if she wasn't in their cabin... that's where she'd be.

James stumbled through the last thicket, breath ragged, heartbeat thunderous in his chest. The old cabin finally emerged through the pale fog like a relic dredged up from memory dark, aged timbers shrouded in morning mist, the roof sagging like a tired sigh. The clearing around it was unnervingly quiet. No birdsong. No breeze. Just silence thick enough to press against the skin.

His boots hit the clearing's edge, breath catching. Please be here. Please...

"Leena?" he called out again, voice barely above a whisper this time. Afraid. Not of ghosts, not of whatever haunted these woods afraid of not hearing her voice call back.

He stepped closer, hand brushing the cabin's weathered siding. The door stood slightly ajar. Cold air whispered out through the crack like an exhale.

He pushed it open.

Inside, dust hung motionless in the thin rays of light piercing through the roof. The same timeworn furniture. The same chill. His eyes scanned for movement, for any sign of her clothes, her sweater, her scent in the air. Nothing.

His boot hit something soft near the door her scarf, bunched like it had been dropped. He picked it up, fingers trembling.

Then something pulled his attention toward the back.

He moved with quiet urgency through the room, stepping over sagging floorboards, turning the corner toward the bedroom.

The room was dim, the air even colder than the rest of the cabin. His flashlight beam skated across the floor landing on it.

There was the open space near the wall. The loosened panel.

And the faintest impression of someone having sat there recently, smoothed fabric still retaining the ghost of her shape.

She'd been here.

James turned slowly, heart sinking with both relief and rising dread. She was alive. But she was deeper in this than he thought. Not just reading Eva's words she was carrying them with her now. Carving them into herself.

That's when he saw it.

The stain. That terrible, rust-colored bloom still soaking the floor. Time hadn't erased it, but he didn't remember seeing it every other time he'd been here.

"Leena!" he called again, louder, desperation thick in his voice.

Then beep.

His body twisted at the sound, heart leaping to his throat.

And in the far corner of the room, curled in on herself like a ghost from another life, was Leena.

Knees to her chest. Eyes wide. Paler than he'd ever seen her.

She looked up at him as if seeing him from a dream she hadn't wanted to wake from.

He dropped to the floor, crawling to her on instinct, breath caught somewhere between sob and relief.

"Leena," he whispered, reaching out but not yet touching. "God, you scared me. I've got you. I'm here."

Her lips parted, but no words came. Only tears. Only silence. Only a forest holding its breath around them once again.

And this time, he didn't let her go.

Chapter 17

They walked back to their cabin in silence, the forest filtering sunlight down through a canopy of leaves. It dappled across their faces and shoulders, painting them with a warmth they didn't quite feel yet. James kept one arm wrapped tightly around Leena, not willing to let her drift even a single inch from him not after what just happened, not after that silence she had curled up into.

She didn't say much. She didn't need to. Her fingers lightly gripping his wrist where his arm circled her waist spoke volumes.

The woods, once eerie and whispering with ghost stories, now simply watched them. The air still carried that faint charge, like the static before a storm, but it was less sharp now. Muted. As if the forest knew this wasn't the time to push them only to let them breathe.

Their boots pressed into the damp earth, leaving a soft trail in the loam. Insects buzzed, and birds dared to sing again, timid notes like the world tiptoeing back to normal. The crunch of leaves beneath their steps, the distant gurgle of the lake, the soft brushing of pine boughs overhead it all became the only sound between them.

The cabin came into view like a haven from another lifetime. Still quiet. Still standing. A piece of their world untouched.

James opened the door for her like it was sacred, like crossing the threshold too quickly might tear the fragile stitching between then and now. She stepped in, let the door shut behind them with a soft click, and leaned her forehead against the wall as if trying to ground herself.

"I couldn't hear anything in there," she finally whispered, voice hoarse. "Not even myself."

James didn't speak. He just moved behind her, wrapping both arms around her from behind, pressing his face into her hair.

"You don't have to explain," he said. "But you're here now. That's enough."

She nodded.

They sat together for a while on the couch, wrapped in the thick quiet of a place that had witnessed far too much. James kept her close, his thumb tracing lazy circles into her shoulder, mentally securing both of them. She leaned into him, her head tucked under his chin, eyes heavy from the weight of what she'd seen what she still couldn't quite put into words.

Eventually, when the sun had sunk low enough to paint the room in soft hues, James stood and quietly made tea. Leena didn't let go of the bundle of letters she'd found. She just held them in her lap, staring at the twine now frayed from use. She would read them again. Not tonight. But soon.

And James, as he stood there watching her from the kitchen, knew something had shifted. She had gone somewhere he couldn't follow. Not fully. But he could wait.

He would wait as long as it took.

She didn't speak right away. Her fingers moved over the frayed twine like they were braiding memory into something more manageable. But after a long moment, she looked up at James, eyes glassy, her voice a rasp barely above a whisper.

"I didn't hear voices," she began, slowly, "but… something was there. Watching. Like the air had weight to it, like I was trespassing in someone else's grief." She looked down at the letters in her lap. "It wasn't fear exactly, but… sadness. Thick. Tangled. I felt like if I spoke, I'd unravel."

James came over with two mugs of tea and set them down gently on the coffee table. He sat beside her and reached for her hand. She took it.

"I thought maybe Eva wanted to show me something," she continued. "There were these letters more than what I found before. They were hidden. Like… like even the walls were trying to forget them." Her voice cracked. "She was unraveling, James. One page at a time. And I think I think a part of me started unraveling too."

James nodded but didn't rush to respond. He thumbed gently over the back of her hand, letting her speak when she was ready.

"She kept writing to him," Leena whispered, "long after she knew he was gone. Not just letters, pleas. She thought maybe if she wrote enough, the forest would answer. That maybe the trees or the wind would carry her words to him."

She turned toward him, her lip trembling. "Have you ever loved someone so much you'd beg the wind for their voice back?"

James's throat closed. But he nodded. "Yeah," he said quietly. "I have."

They sat there, the weight of unsaid things settling between them. not heavy, but very real.

"You don't have to carry this alone," James said after a while. "Whatever is happening out there whatever did happen… we're in it together now."

She managed a small smile, tired and grateful. "I know."

Wanting to pull her gently from the edge of whatever darkness she'd brought back with her, James leaned closer and brushed his nose against her temple.

"Hey," he said softly, nudging her. "You know, I had this whole plan today. I was gonna pretend we were normal, make food, maybe fail spectacularly at chopping wood again."

She gave a small huff of laughter. "You chop wood like a city boy."

"I am a city boy."

"Explains the band-aids on your thumbs."

They smiled at each other real smiles this time. Small. Earned. Cracked around the edges. But honest.

"Let's just exist tonight," James said. "No ghosts, letters. Just us."

She leaned into him, resting her head on his shoulder. "That sounds perfect."

And for the first time in days, the cabin felt like theirs again not just borrowed space wrapped in someone else's tragedy. The past lingered, yes. The woods still watched, yes. But for this small flicker of time, they had each other.

The silence that followed wasn't heavy it was delicate, like the moment after a wish is spoken. James moved back to the couch, nudging Leena with a crooked smile. "So," he said gently, "are we just going to keep sitting here until one of us turns into furniture?"

She snorted, just a little, the first real sound of amusement that had escaped her since they returned. "Maybe. Could be the only way I finally relax."

"Or," James offered, voice light, "we could do something productive. Like... make popcorn and argue over which movie aged better Howard the duck or The Princess Bride."

She tilted her head, feigning scandal. "You dare bring The Princess Bride into this sacred space?"

He leaned in, mock-serious. "You wound me, madam."

Laughter bubbled up between them. A soothing quiet promise.

It started with a smile and a gentle kiss just a press of lips to lips. But smiles deepened, kisses lingered, hands found familiar curves with unfamiliar hunger.

They didn't speak. They didn't need to. It was all there in the way they held each other, in the way Leena buried her face in his neck, in the way James gripped her like a man coming up for air.

After, tangled on the couch beneath a blanket pulled from the back of it. Leena's breathing evened, her fingers tucked gently into the crook of James's arm. She fell asleep like that bare, vulnerable, home.

But James stayed awake.

He watched the fire flicker low. The letters sat forgotten on the table. The night was quiet, too quiet, and yet he didn't feel afraid. Not exactly. Only thoughtful. Aware.

His mind replayed the day the forest, the blood, the light, the way she had looked when he found her. And now, here. Whole, resting.

He tucked a strand of hair behind her ear and exhaled slowly.

"I've got you," he whispered into her hair, voice barely audible.

Enough to hold them together through the weight of everything left unspoken. Enough to keep the ghosts at bay. Enough to remind them that even though the road had cracked and broken under them, they were still here scarred, stitched, and breathing.

The fire had faded to a faint orange glow, its light dancing like a memory on the walls. Leena stirred slightly in her sleep, shifting just enough for James to wrap the blanket tighter around her shoulders. He watched her chest rise and fall in rhythm, the steady cadence letting him know he was somewhere safe.

His fingers grazed over her knuckles, memorizing them again. All the jagged pieces of their past had somehow brought them to this quiet cabin in the woods brought them face-to-face with not just the truth of each other, but the stories that lingered in the timber, in the pages of long-forgotten journals, in the blood rusted into the floorboards.

James leaned back into the couch cushion and let his eyes wander the room. Everything felt older tonight. Heavier, almost as if they were somewhere time folded in on itself. Where you couldn't tell if you were dreaming or simply remembering too vividly.

Something about this place remembered stories

It held them close, replayed them, whispered them back into hearts like his and hers.

He looked down at Leena again, brushing his lips to her forehead. A gesture. A vow.

They had seen something ancient in these woods. Something human. Something holy. And if that meant their love had to be carved out between haunted echoes and unfinished stories, then so be it.

He could bear it.

With her, he could bear anything.

And as sleep finally crept toward him, curling slow and warm through his limbs, he swore he heard something outside the window. Not a howl. Not the wind.

A hum.

Soft. Familiar.

Like someone humming a lullaby from long, long ago.

*beep

Chapter 18

The morning light filtered lazily through the windows of the cabin, painting soft golden squares on the floor. Both James and Leena had slept in, the tension of the past days finally settling just enough to allow their bodies a deeper rest. The air was heavy with the scent of wood, rich and earthy, their movements remained slow, almost cautious, as if speaking too loudly might break whatever fragile calm they had found.

James stretched first, walking barefoot across the creaky floor toward the kitchen. Leena emerged a few moments later, wrapped in one of his flannels, her hair a disheveled halo around her face. Their eyes met, and something flickered there recognition, comfort, the faintest spark of amusement.

"How about a better day?" James asked, handing her a steaming mug.

She took it, fingers brushing his. "Sure, but don't try to make me do anything."

He chuckled. "No promises."

They shared breakfast in quiet companionship, the occasional grin or teasing glance easing them into something like normal. It was a tense kind of normal, sure but normal nonetheless. The kind that couples on the mend cling to like driftwood.

By late morning, they decided to go into town again. Supplies were low, and neither of them had any desire to cook. They drove in mostly silence, the occasional soft hum from the radio filling the car like white noise.

Halfway to town, Leena's phone beeped. Just once. No messages. No alerts. Just the sound. James glanced at her.

"Again?" he asked.

She nodded, eyes narrowed. "Yeah. It's weird."

"Maybe it just misses civilization."

"Or maybe the forest is trying to subscribe to my Spotify."

They both laughed, and just like that, the weight in the air lifted.

When they reached town, the streets were as charmingly quiet as before. The same locals sat outside the diner, and the same retro music wafted through the cracked door. They stepped inside, greeted by the familiar chime of the bell and the warm scent of fresh pies.

"Your booth's open," the waitress said with a wink, recognizing them instantly. "Glad to see you two again."

Leena smiled and slid into the vinyl seat across from James.

"This place is starting to feel like our portal to normal," she murmured.

James grinned. "Portal to grease and pie, yes please."

They ordered the same meals as last time, letting the comfort of repetition soothe whatever ghost had followed them from the woods. Between bites of his burger, James leaned forward.

"I was thinking," he said, "maybe we come back here when we're old and gray. Make this our thing. Diner dates. Bad coffee. Your laugh echoing off retro tile."

Leena raised a brow. "You're planning a lot of years into the future for someone who still hasn't unpacked his bag."

He grinned. "Well, I figure if I lock you in with food and nostalgia, I've got a chance."

As if on cue, the jukebox crooned out It's Been a Long, Long Time, and Leena reached across the table to squeeze his hand.

"No Peggy jokes this time?" she teased.

James leaned in, eyes bright. "You kidding? That's too easy. I was gonna say something much smoother. Like... you're the only time traveler I'd let wreck my whole timeline."

She laughed full, genuine. The sound turned heads and made the waitress chuckle behind the counter.

"You're both adorable," the woman said as she passed.

They lingered long after the plates were cleared, sipping coffee and sharing quiet glances. The beep came again. Soft. Subtle. Like it had always been part of the song.

But they didn't let it shake them. Not today.

After lunch, they wandered the little shops, picking up odds and ends they didn't truly need but wanted anyway. A candle that smelled like cinnamon. A notebook with a hand-stitched cover. A silly postcard of a bear in a bathtub.

They walked hand in hand back to the car as the sun dipped lower behind the trees.

"Today was good," James said.

"Yeah," Leena agreed. "It really was."

As they drove back to the cabin, the trees seemed to part a little easier. The forest, for now, content to let them be.

They stopped once along the way, the gravel crunching beneath their tires as they pulled off onto a quiet overlook. The valley stretched below them, kissed by the soft gold of evening light. Mountains stood in solemn vigil, treetops waving like green oceans beneath a sleepy sky. They didn't speak at first just stood side by side, the breeze threading through their fingers.

Leena leaned her head on James's shoulder. "Do you think it's possible," she said softly, "to fall in love with the same person all over again?"

He looked at her, eyes tracing the outline of her face, the wind lifting her hair in gentle wisps.

"I think I've been doing it every day since we got here."

She smiled, and finally, it didn't feel fragile.

He pressed a kiss to her temple, then tucked her under his arm. "We'll be okay, won't we?"

She didn't answer right away. Just slid her hand into his. "We already are."

As they got back into the car, the radio clicked on by itself, static humming before fading into a familiar tune. Another glitch. Or maybe not. They didn't acknowledge it.

They drove the rest of the way in companionable silence, fingers intertwined over the gearshift, the sky deepening above them.

And when the cabin came into view, warm light glowing from the windows like a heartbeat, they both let out the breath they hadn't known they were holding.

Inside, the cabin was warm with the residual heat from the sun-soaked logs and the slow-burning fire James had tended earlier. They didn't bother turning on any lights just the amber flicker from the hearth casting their shadows in a lazy dance across the wooden walls. James nudged the record player to life again, the crackle of vinyl rising before an old jazz number filled the space.

Leena twirled once dramatically across the room, her socks sliding on the worn wooden floor. "Careful," James laughed, "that's how hips get broken after thirty."

She spun around to him, grinning. "Then catch me, old man."

"Oh, is that how it is?" He reached for her waist with mock offense. "You think I won't sweep you off your feet?"

"I know you will. But then we'll both end up on the floor. And your pride doesn't bounce."

James pulled her into his arms anyway, her laughter muffled against his chest. They danced, not to the beat of the song, but to the rhythm only they could feel cheek to cheek, slow and swaying, whispering ridiculous things and stolen promises.

"You know," James murmured, "I think if I met you for the first time right now, I'd still fall for you in five seconds flat."

She pulled back just enough to look him in the eyes. "Even with all this baggage?"

He leaned his forehead against hers. "Especially because of it. Its ours anyway
The music played on. She kissed him slow, the kind of kiss that only

happens when you know what it is to lose something and get it back by grace alone.

They collapsed onto the couch in a heap of giggles and tangled limbs, like teenagers after curfew, hearts full of too much everything. Pillows fell. Her hair was a mess. His shirt was half unbuttoned. None of it mattered.

Until the beep came again.

Sharp. Artificial. Jarring.

Leena sat up, breathless and annoyed. "Seriously?"

James froze. "Was that "

"Yes. Again."

They both stared at the phone sitting innocently on the end table.

"No message. No call. No nothing. Just that sound." She stood, scooped the phone up, and held it in both hands like she might throw it into the fire. "I've had it."

James raised an eyebrow. "You gonna throw it outside?"

"Something like that." She held the power button down until the screen went dark, black as ink. "There. Dead. Maybe now it'll shut up."

"Or it becomes haunted and passive-aggressive," James said, grinning. "Let's hope it doesn't start whispering tonight."

Leena tossed the phone onto the counter and returned to the couch, flopping dramatically into his arms.
"If it does, you're sleeping closest to it."

"I knew if pressed you'd use me as ghost bait."

She smirked, then softened, her fingertips tracing the lines of his jaw. "You'd survive. You've got that heroic jawline. Classic final boss."

"Oh, is that what's keeping me alive? Not my sparkling wit?"

"Nope. Just the jaw."

They both laughed again, the sound echoing softly in the rafters.

Outside, the wind rustled the trees. Inside, two souls who had almost lost each other played and joked like no one was watching because finally, in this quiet stretch of forest wrapped in mystery and second chances no one was.

The hush of evening falling soft over the roof line. The crickets had started singing again tentative at first, like testing the weight of peace. Leena's hair, carrying the faintest hint of woodsmoke and pine. Her face was pressed against James's chest, and for a few moments, they didn't speak. They just stood there, rotating, holding each other like a shield against the world.

James exhaled, one of those long, heavy breaths that meant something meant this is what I've been needing. His chin rested on the crown of her head. She felt warm, real.

"Do you remember," he whispered, "how i used to try to dance just on the side of the road?"

She nodded against him. "You always stepped on my toes."

"that was to make you laugh," he added.

"Thats a weird way to do it"

He kissed her forehead. "We can get that back."

"We are getting it back," she said, voice so soft it nearly disappeared into the night air.

The porch light flickered slightly just a hiccup and neither of them noticed.

Or maybe they just didn't care.

Inside, the record player had spun to silence, but they kept dancing, swaying, shifting weight from foot to foot. James reached behind her and opened the door with one hand, keeping her close with the other. They stumbled in without letting go, their laughter soft, giddy. Leena toed the door shut behind them, sealing them into a moment that felt untouched by time or fear.

She turned in his arms and tilted her head. "So," she said, grinning, "are we the weird cabin couple now?"

James smirked. "Maybe buy you start naming squirrels, I'm pulling the plug."
"Too late. Gerald already lives under the porch."

He groaned, falling with her onto the bed. "We're doomed."

"Doomed," she agreed, curling into him, "and deliriously happy."

They kissed again, lazy and warm. His thumb traced lines on her shoulder as her hand found his heartbeat. They didn't need to say it out loud how much they had both feared this would never be theirs again. They didn't need to name the ache or the ghosts.

They were healing and still writing their story.
The only sound for a while was the crackling of the fire, the quiet rhythm of breathing, the gentle hush of two people rediscovering everything they once lost.

Until

*beep.

It cut through the stillness like a pin dropped in an empty room.

Leena flinched against him. James's arm tensed.
They didn't move. Didn't look.
"I turned it off," she murmured.

"I know," James said.

They waited a beat longer, the fire popping in the hearth.

Then Leena pulled the throw blanket tighter around them and whispered, "I'm not scared."

James nodded, kissing her temple again. "Me neither."

And just like that, the silence swallowed the sound.

Like the trees outside, like the stories buried in roots and ruins and journals worn with time. Waiting.

But for now, Leena and James had each other, wrapped in laughter and shadow and the long, slow miracle of starting again.

And in that flickering warmth, they didn't just feel safe.
it was a reaffirming wakening, that the cracks finally started to fill in.

Chapter 19

James woke slowly.

The bed was cold beside him.

No scent of coffee. No quiet hum of the record player. No sound of water boiling on the stove.

Just stillness.

He sat up, heart knocking unevenly in his chest. The cabin felt different emptier somehow, like the walls were holding their breath. He called her name once, then again, a little louder.

Nothing.

His feet hit the floor with a thud, every step creaking through the wood. The silence pressed in from all sides.

And Leena was completely gone.

The coffee pot was untouched. Her phone was still on the counter, the screen dark. A shiver threaded through his spine as he crossed the room to the windows, peering out into the forest. The trees swayed gently, sunlight cutting through in slanted rays but there was no movement. No sign of her.

He grabbed his boots, pulling them on in a rush. His hands trembled as he laced them, already imagining worst-case scenarios. She wouldn't just leave. Not without saying something. Not after everything they'd been through.

Outside, the air was crisp, the remnants of morning dew still clinging to the grass. He scanned the treeline, hoping to see her figure emerge from the shadows with a sheepish grin and a sarcastic remark. But there was only the sound of wind whispering through the pines.

He tried the lake path first. It was the most obvious her favorite spot to think. But the dock was empty, the surface of the water undisturbed. He stood at the edge, breath heavy, mind racing.

Then, faint and sudden a beep.

He turned sharply, eyes scanning the woods behind him.

"Leena?" he called, voice raw.

No answer.

He ran. Through the trees. Down the trails they knew. He shouted for her, again and again, hoping to hear her voice call back. But the forest swallowed every sound.

He reached the old cabin and burst through the door.

Empty.

The floorboards groaned beneath his weight. He checked every room, calling her name with increasing desperation. But she wasn't there. She wasn't anywhere.

James stood in the center of the room, breathing hard. His pulse echoed in his ears. A knot formed in his chest, pulling tight.

She was gone.

Not just missing for a moment, gone.

And she had left everything behind.

The weight of it dropped onto his shoulders like stone.

He fell to his knees, hands gripping the edge of the table, head bowed.

He didn't know if she had gone willingly or not. If she was following something, chasing something, escaping something. But she was gone.

And now, he was alone.

In a cabin full of ghosts and stories that had never finished being told.

He slumped back onto his heels, trying to trace her movements like footprints in his memory. Had she said something the night before? Left a sign? A message? He thought of every look, every word, every silence wondering if he'd missed something vital.

There had to be something.

Rushing back to their cabin his thoughts were a fog of what-ifs and should-haves. He stumbled upright, pacing like a caged animal, fingers twitching against his sides as his eyes scanned the room for clues that didn't exist. Her boots were still by the door. Her jacket hung on the back of the chair. The blanket they curled up under the night before still held the shape of her body.

And yet it was as if she'd been peeled out of the world, plucked from it like a loose thread pulled clean from a tapestry.
He opened cabinets. Pulled drawers. Looked under pillows. Behind furniture. He wasn't even sure what he was looking for just anything. Something.

Her absence wasn't just physical. It was loud. Screaming in the silence, rattling through the floorboards. He wandered out onto the porch, the wood groaning beneath him, and stared out at the trees. They looked the same. Still and quiet. No signs of struggle. No footprints in the damp earth.

Just that relentless silence.

A part of him whispered that maybe maybe she had gone back to town. Maybe she needed time. Space. But that part of him was quickly buried under the reality that she would've said something. Written something. And she hadn't.

And that beep…

He closed his eyes. It echoed now in his skull. That disembodied digital noise in a place with no reception. No signal. He hadn't imagined it.

Or maybe he had.

He sank onto the edge of the porch, elbows on his knees, fingers threaded through his hair.

He'd never been more terrified in his life.

Worse than the night they fought until the walls could've split. Worse than the moment he confessed what he'd done and watched her eyes go glassy with betrayal. This was something else. This was emptiness.

And still no clue. No sign. Just the cruel warmth of the morning sun, burning through the chill in the air like nothing had changed like the universe didn't notice she was gone.

He stood abruptly, the sudden movement making him dizzy. He

needed to move. He needed to do something. Standing still was drowning him.

Back inside the cabin, he checked her phone again. Still off. No new alerts. No signal bars. Just that blank screen.

The air felt stale again. Heavy. Like it hadn't been breathed in hours.

He grabbed his coat and headed for the woods. Not in any specific direction. Just away. Somewhere. Anywhere that might let him think. Might let him understand.

Every step into the trees felt like stepping through a veil. The forest seemed to close around him soft pine needles underfoot, the hush of wind in the branches, the occasional snap of something in the underbrush. But nothing human. Nothing familiar.

Just nature. Watching.

He stopped at the edge of the path they'd walked a hundred times before and let out a breath so deep it shook.

"I don't know what you want," he whispered to the trees. "But you can't have her. You can't just take her."

No response. Just wind.

He thought of the stories. Of Eva and Wren. Of the flickering light. Of the beeps. The way this place seemed to listen. To lure. And for the first time in days, he let himself feel the weight of fear that had been building under the surface.

What if this wasn't just another fight?
What if the woods had taken her?
What if they never gave her back?

He turned in a slow circle, scanning the trees, hoping praying for a flash of her face, her hair, anything to anchor him back to her. But there was only green and brown and sky. And silence.

James dropped to his knees on the path, the weight of everything finally pressing him to the earth.

"I'm not leaving without you," he said into the wind. "Do you hear me? I'll burn this whole forest to the ground if that's what it takes."

The wind shifted. Leaves rustled. But no answer came.

Only that silence.

Still, he didn't move.

Because even though she was gone James wasn't. Not yet.
And as long as he was still breathing, he would keep searching.
He would tear the woods apart, one tree at a time.

But then he stopped.

What if she came back?

What if she was already on her way through some winding trail, or from the lake's far edge and he left in a blind panic, only for her to find the cabin empty?

His breath hitched. The thought made his stomach turn.

What if she returned, needing him, and he wasn't there?
Running back. He gripped the door frame with both hands and stared into the trees as if they could give him an answer. They only whispered back in rustling indifference.

Town. Should he go to town? Ask around? Maybe she'd hitched a ride with one of the rare hikers who passed through. Maybe she'd gone for help. Maybe maybe maybe. Each theory flickered across his mind like lightning, but none stuck. None made sense.

No coat. No boots. No phone.

And no goodbye.

The silence in the cabin was unbearable. It draped across the space like an abandoned memory. The only sound was the ticking of the old clock above the mantle a slow, steady mockery of time's unfeeling march forward.

He walked to the table and sat, hands trembling, the weight of indecision pressing hard on his chest.

Leave… and she might return to no one.

Stay… and what if she needed him?

He clenched his jaw, pressing the heel of his palm into his eye socket, fighting off the ache blooming behind his eyes. "God, Leena… where the hell are you?"

Another minute passed.

Then another.

His legs wouldn't stay still. He stood. Paced. Sat again. Every inch of the cabin now felt wrong. Crooked. Like the walls were tilting just slightly inward. Her absence created a vacuum like her laughter had been the thing holding this place upright.

The firewood still lay by the door where he had dropped it the morning before.

Half-split logs.

No fire.

No warmth.

He crossed to the window and opened it, letting the late summer air roll over his skin. It smelled of pine needles and faint smoke in the distance somewhere, someone was burning leaves.

She'd have said it smelled like memory.

She always had words for things he couldn't name.

"Where did you go?" he whispered to the forest. It didn't answer.

He glanced to the counter where her phone still sat, face down, lifeless.

His own was in his pocket. He pulled it out. No signal. Useless.

He stared at the screen like it owed him an explanation. And just as he thought it, the device beeped.

That damn beep again.

He flinched, nearly dropping it.

No messages. No notifications. No call.

Just that sound.

He shut it off.

His gaze swept over the inside of the cabin once more. He hadn't missed anything. There was nothing new. No fresh footprint. No hastily scrawled note. The same scarf still hung by the door. Her sweater still draped over the couch.

Everything was where it had been.

Except her.

He walked back to the bedroom, sat on the edge of the bed they'd shared so full of whispered words and tangled promises and now it felt like a tomb. Still warm, barely. His hand brushed over the pillow where her head had rested just hours ago.

The indentation was fading.

A knock of panic rattled deep in his chest.

He stood again and grabbed his jacket from the chair.

If he didn't move, he'd drown in the stillness.

But no decision felt right.

The woods called to him. But so did the cabin. The hope however small that she'd walk through the door with an explanation, a laugh, a Leena-style dismissal of concern. I was just out walking, you big idiot. Calm down.

But the longer he waited, the less likely it felt.

James stepped to the threshold of the cabin again.

And this time, he stayed there one foot inside, one foot out.
Suspended in the in-between.
Not willing to risk losing her twice.

But he couldn't just wait.

"Screw it," he muttered, grabbing her sketchpad off the table.

He tore out a page and scrawled a note in his messy, shaking hand:

I'm going to town. If you come back please, stay.

He folded the note and set it under the ceramic mug she always used, placing it square in the center of the table.

With a final glance around the cabin that already felt too quiet, too empty, James grabbed his coat and stepped out the door.

He didn't look back.

The road to town was long and winding. But he had to try. He had to believe that somewhere, somehow, she was out there

He drove cautiously, scanning the woods, the road looking for every little hint.

The road stretched endlessly before him, but everything felt… off. Trees leaned differently. Curves in the road seemed just a little too sharp, or not sharp enough. The signs he swore should be there were gone. He checked the dash same gas level, same flickering clock. He hadn't missed a turn.

But the world around him felt shifted. Tilted.

He pressed harder on the gas.

He should've seen the diner by now. The warm flicker of neon lights. The sleepy hum of a place that never really changed. The old signs nailed to trees. That crooked bench outside where Leena had once rested her head against his shoulder.

But it wasn't there.

The clearing where the town should've begun was swallowed in mist. Pale, thick fog rolled in with an unnatural slowness, blanketing everything in a dull, silver-gray sheen. Trees stood in its haze like gaunt sentinels. No birds. No sound.

No town.
James hit the brakes, tires crunching against gravel.

"What the hell…"

He leaned forward, squinting through the windshield. The road was still there technically. But the curve ahead that usually opened up to Main Street was gone. Just more trees. His headlights.
They barely cut through the fog.

Panic began to claw at his chest. He reached for the radio static. No signal. His phone? Still no bars. No GPS. Nothing.

Just dead space.

He turned off the engine and sat in the silence, hands gripping the steering wheel like it should just anchor him in a world that suddenly didn't feel real.

This was the way to town. He knew it.

He'd driven it with her plenty of times. The same hills, the same curves, the same shoulder where they pulled over once to watch the stars. He could still smell the damn cheeseburgers from the diner if he closed his eyes.

So where was it?

Why did everything look the same… but not?

A dull beep cut through the stillness.

His head snapped toward the sound but it wasn't in the car. It came from somewhere deeper in the trees.

The sound wasn't supposed to come here.

"Leena?" He whispered to the fog.

No response.

He opened the door slowly and stepped out, boots crunching on the loose gravel. The cold bit at his skin. He took a few hesitant steps forward, peering into the endless gray ahead.

The trees looked older somehow. Twisted. Their branches heavy with damp, clinging moss. Everything smelled of wet earth and silence.

He didn't dare walk into the fog.

Not yet.

But the diner should've been here. The gas station. The cracked Coca-Cola sign. The hum of a town that had lived through decades.

Gone.

Swallowed whole.
Like it never existed.

James backed up slowly, heart pounding in his ears.

The woods didn't just feel like they were watching.

They felt like they had shifted.

Bent themselves just enough to keep him locked inside some version of a memory. A warped version of reality where the exit signs were written in smoke and old echoes.

*beep

He turned back toward the car, slid in, and slammed the door.
He wasn't sure whether to scream or laugh.
Where the hell was he?
Where the hell was she?

As his thoughts started to sharpen, maybe in his panic he didn't go far enough. "That has to be it" "Ill go a little bit farther." and with that he dropped the car into gear and headed into the fog.

Chapter 20

The town never came.

The road unfurled before him in that winding, familiar way except it wasn't familiar anymore. The turns were too tight, the shadows deeper. Even the trees lining the shoulder seemed to lean different-ly, like they were watching him, whispering to one another.

He checked the GPS. No signal. The screen flickered, then went black.

He cursed under his breath, glanced at the rear-view mirror like the world behind him might've made more sense. But it didn't.

Still, he pushed forward.

Another bend. Another mile.

Where the hell was the diner? The old hardware store? The rusting mailbox shaped like a trout that marked the halfway point?

Gone.

Vanished.

"Where the hell is the goddamn town?" he hissed.

Then beep.

He slammed the brakes.

The tires locked and the car skidded to a stop in the middle of the road.

The beep hadn't come from his phone it was off. He hadn't heard that sound inside the car. It had come from everywhere. Inside. Outside. A glitch in the world that pressed its claws just behind his eardrum.

He screamed loud, furious, hopeless. The kind that came from the deepest part of a man unraveling.

And then he spun the car around.

The fog was thick now. It hadn't been that thick before.

Branches scraped against the windows like fingernails. The head-lights stretched into the fog, but offered no answers.
James gritted his teeth and drove.

Fast.

Back the way he came.
Back toward the one place that still held any meaning.
Back to the cabin.

He tore down the gravel lane, headlights bouncing over the uneven terrain. Every pothole rattled his bones, every shadow fed the dread ballooning in his chest.

And when the cabin finally emerged through the fog, dark and hunched against the hillside, it didn't feel like relief.

It felt like a dare.

He flung the car door open and ran up the steps, stumbling over himself in the rush.

He burst through the front door.

"Leena!"

Silence.

Just like before.

The note still sat on the table, untouched beneath her favorite mug.

His breath came in harsh, uneven gasps. The air inside the cabin was colder now unwelcoming.

*beep.

He spun, eyes wild, scanning the corners.

The sound had come from nowhere. And everywhere.

And it was driving him mad.

He collapsed into the couch, elbows on his knees, hands gripping his hair. Sweat beaded at his temple despite the chill.

"Come on, baby. Where are you?" he whispered.

Outside, the trees swayed too gently. Too slowly.

The cabin didn't feel like home anymore.

It felt like a mouth.

Waiting to close.

The cabin was too quiet.

James stood in the middle of the room, chest heaving. He'd made it back from the failed drive to town, where reality itself had bent in all the wrong ways. And now, standing here alone the weight of her absence pressed down like a second gravity.

No note. No clue. Just that sketchpad, now closed and sitting where he left it, and a cold air inside that hadn't been there before.

He paced.
Back and forth.
Again.
Again.

Each turn growing more manic, his mind circling the same useless questions. Where had she gone? Why? How could someone disappear so cleanly, so silently, without even the grace of a slammed door or a final word?

His fingers ran through his hair, pulling hard.

*beep.

He froze.

Not again.

It came from the corner of the room or the ceiling? Or from inside him? It was impossible to place, high-pitched and wrong, like a dying battery or a mocking ghost.

"Leena?" he called again, already knowing it was useless.

Nothing answered.

James clenched his jaw so hard it ached. His fists pounded the table once, twice, until the ceramic mug toppled over and shattered.

The sound startled him. And then he laughed. A sharp, hollow sound.

"What do you want from me?" he shouted to the ceiling, to the walls, to the woods themselves. "You took her, now what?"

*beep.

He spun, eyes darting like a predator, searching for something any-thing to fight.

Then the room went still again. The only sound was his ragged breathing.

The fire had long since died. Ashes in the hearth. Shadows curled in the corners like sleeping dogs.

James dropped to his knees in front of the fireplace, bracing himself with one hand on the cold stone. The other trembled uselessly at his side.

She was gone.

And now the place they'd come to heal felt like it was swallowing him whole.

He didn't know how long he sat there, until his limbs went numb and the ache in his chest quieted to a dull hum.

He stood slowly, dragging himself to the bathroom. He splashed cold water on his face, stared into the mirror at a version of himself that barely looked human anymore. Hollow-eyed. Haunted.

When he stepped back into the main room, it hit again beep.

Louder this time.

Closer.

He turned and hurled her phone across the room. It shattered against the wall.

He collapsed onto the couch, gripping a throw pillow to his chest like a life raft.

Maybe this was the price of everything. Of the love. The pain. The truths never spoken until it was too late.

The cabin was no longer sanctuary.
It was a cage.

And that sound the beep it was the key, turning slowly the lock.

James curled into himself, eyes wide and staring into the dark beyond the flickering light of the of the room. He didn't cry.

He didn't even blink.

The cabin was no longer a shelter.
It pulsed with absence.

James paced like a animal. The only rhythm now was the beep no longer a gentle beep, but a mechanical, taunting sound. Not from anything he could see. It came from nowhere and everywhere, low and electronic, like some tear in the fabric of reality.

Beep.
Silence.
Beep.
Silence.
Like a countdown.

He clutched at his hair, chest heaving. The fireplace, the books, the journals it all meant nothing without her here. The couch still smelled like her. The sheets held the shape of her sleep. But she was gone.

And something wanted him to know it.

He turned toward the window.

That's when he saw it.

A flicker. Just past the tree line. Pale and ghostlike, not fire, not flashlight. It shimmered briefly like a candle underwater, then faded but James was already moving.

He yanked open the door, boots crashing through the brush. The cold air slapped his face, but he didn't stop to grab a jacket. He didn't care. Not anymore.

"Leena!" he bellowed into the trees.

The forest gave no reply.

Branches clawed at his arms, roots bit into his ankles, but James pushed forward. His lungs burned. His pulse was a roar in his ears. That light he had seen it. He knew what he saw.

He kept his eyes locked on the space where it had flickered.

The hairs on the back of his neck stood up.

This wasn't her, but it was calling him.

And like a idiot he obeyed.

The woods were different now. The trees older, tighter together, crowding him like silent witnesses. The sky overhead dimmed, though it was barely night.

He stumbled over a fallen log, fell hard on his side, cursed, and got back up.

Mud smeared down his arm. A branch had torn a line across his cheek. He didn't care. All he could hear was that beep.

All he could see was her face, blurred by panic and memory.

Where did you go?

He broke into a small clearing. Heart pounding. Chest heaving.

Nothing.

Only trees. Shadows. The wind.

Then movement.

To the left.

He spun, catching it the light again. This time higher, like it floated just above eye level. And then it moved deeper into the trees. Slow. Deliberate. Waiting for him to follow.

And James ran.

He chased it, branches ripping into his face, his breath ragged. His mind a storm. The forest bent and stretched around him, the light always just out of reach, blinking like a warning.

Beep.

Like a countdown to something ancient, something sacred, or maybe damned.

He didn't stop until the light vanished completely.

And there in the dark he realized he was far. Too far.

Nothing looked familiar. The trail behind him had vanished. Even the trees looked like strangers.

For the first time, James stopped.

His hands trembled at his sides. His breath steamed in the air. The weight of everything dropped into his stomach.

He wasn't alone. But not in a good way.

He turned slowly, scanning the dark.

"Leena?" he whispered again. But it was a hope spoken into oblivion.
And the only answer that came.....*beep

The forest swallowed him.

Darkness had finally settled, dense and absolute. The trees pressed in close thick with moss and cold silence and James was broken in the center of it all.

The fall had come fast.
One misplaced step chasing after the light, and he'd plummeted through brush and roots and jagged stone. His ankle had twisted first, then something harder caught his shoulder, and his side slammed into a downed tree with the unforgiving thud of reality.

But he hadn't stopped.
Not at first.

Adrenaline was a liar. It whispered strength where there was none, hid the damage beneath urgency. He had gotten up, kept moving, shouting for her through clenched teeth and blurry vision.

Chapter 21

Now it all hit.

The pain radiated through him like lightning caught in bone. His ribs ached with every breath. His legs shook with exhaustion and bruised muscle. Blood warm and sticky trailed down from a gash above his eyebrow. He tasted dirt. His hands were scraped raw.

He couldn't even remember falling the second time, but here he was collapsed against the damp forest floor, face to bark, chest heaving, cold biting at his skin. The air was wet. Heavy. Smelling of earth and rot and rain that hadn't yet fallen.

James rolled onto his back, eyes staring up at the ink-dark canopy.

No stars. No moon.

Just black branches like claws against the sky.

His breath hitched.

"Leena…" he croaked. It came out more like a prayer than a name.

He winced, clutching at his ribs. He didn't know if anything was broken, but it didn't matter. He was alone, hurt, and lost. And something deeper than bone was cracking inside him.

Not just fear but grief.

He blinked hard against the tears burning the edges of his vision.

Where was she?

Why did she leave?

And why did it feel like the whole world was conspiring to keep her from him?

The beep came again.

Louder this time.

Not just a beep. Not just distant. But near. Pulsing.

He turned his head slowly, eyes catching movement just past a cluster of ferns. No light now. No guiding glow. Just sound.

He pressed a shaking hand to the ground, trying to sit upright, gasping as his body screamed in protest.

Beep.

He swore under his breath, half-laughing, half-sobbing. "You've got to be fucking kidding me…"

Whatever it was… it wasn't done with him.

He forced himself up. Every motion a war. He leaned against a tree, breath fogging the air, mind running in static loops. If he could just make it back to the cabin back to the place that used to mean safety he could regroup, plan, and search again.

Because no matter what pain screamed through his body…

He wasn't done.

Not until she was back.
Not until the story ended together.
He took one step.

Then another.

Each footfall a personal hell.
But still, he moved.
Through the trees. Through the dark. Through the pain.
Because somewhere out there, Leena had to be waiting.

And if the forest wanted to kill him
It would have to do a hell of a lot more than this.

But the pain was merciless now his joints stiff, his lungs burning
with every breath. His chest felt like it might cave in, but he kept
going. The forest around him was no longer welcoming or even
indifferent. It growled with something else. Something darker. The
trees seemed closer. The shadows heavier. Every footstep was a
scream of muscle and splintered pain shooting everywhere through
his entire body.

The fog began to roll in, curling low and ghostlike around his legs,
winding through the trees like it knew the path better than he did.

That beep no longer a beep was steady now. Mechanical. Methodical. It pressed into his skull, matched the throb in his ankle, the
pounding of his heart.

Then the light appeared again
Flickering. Just beyond the fog. Off the path. Not moving anymore.

It hovered in the dark, waiting.
James froze.

Flashlight trembling in his hand, the sweat on his back gone ice
cold.

The light did not blink or shift. It simply was as if the woods had finally decided to reveal their secret.

He limped one step forward.
Then another.

The light didn't move, it just waited.

And James, broken and desperate, started moving again toward whatever truth lay hidden in the woods.

Every step hurt. His ankle throbbed viciously, each movement sending lances of pain up his leg and into his spine. His breath came in ragged gasps, each inhale slicing through his ribs like ice. The flashlight beam quivered with every stumble, casting shadows that danced like phantoms against the trees.

The forest had changed. The vibrant canopy from days before was swallowed in gray, the pines tall and grave. The fog clung to the ground, soft and silent as death, curling around his legs like something alive. Branches clawed at his jacket, unseen roots threatened to trip him with every step.

The deeper he went, the darker it became.

The beep grew louder. Not in volume, but in presence. It became the rhythm of his heartbeat, the ticking of a countdown he couldn't see.

Ahead, the light remained still and steady.
And then it stopped.
No flicker. No fade.
Just gone again.
James froze.

The forest was silent. The fog held still. The trees loomed like silent guardians but, he was alone again.

And then he felt he wasn't.
Behind the veil of fog, something shifted.
He raised his flashlight.
Nothing.

Only trees, fog, and silence.

His body knew. His blood knew.
Something was there, watching.
The woods… they were listening.

James pressed forward, each breath a fight for survival, every step a vow that he would find her.

Even if he had to die to do it.

James staggered forward, his boots crunching wet leaves and broken twigs.
Breath ragged, pain radiating from his ankle with every forced step. His body was a map of bruises, his palms scraped raw, his ribs aching from the earlier fall but it didn't matter. Not now.

Chapter 22

They started as whispers. Not quite words. Not in any language he recognized. They felt disjointed like echoes from another world. A world layered just beneath this one, brushing against his mind in pulses of memory and noise.

He could make out the voices distinct, overlapping but the meanings refused to settle. They poured over and around him, not into him.

They weren't meant to be understood. Only felt.

His jaw clenched as he stumbled again, catching himself against a trunk slick with moss. "Leena?" he rasped, knowing she wouldn't answer but needing to hear her name out loud.

The light came again glowing brighter now. Ethereal. A silvery white that shimmered like moonlight reflected off ice.

It pulsed not like anything man-made, but like something alive. Ancient, like a presence. It hovered just above the ground, too steady to be a lantern, too fluid to be fire. James blinked, breath catching.

It felt… familiar.

Not from memory but from somewhere deeper. Like a childhood dream he forgot but never stopped yearning for.

His flashlight flickered, then gave up.

Only the glow remained.

It didn't illuminate so much as hush the dark. Like it didn't just push the shadows away it asked them to take a step back.

And the whispers? Still there. Still foreign. But… intimate.

James kept walking. Limping, dragging his breath through clenched teeth. Not because he believed the light would lead him to Leena anymore, just because he had no other direction left.

He didn't know why.

Maybe he was dying.
Maybe this was what the end looked like before the forest finally swallowed him.

The light didn't retreat. It expanded.

Like it was letting him in.

Like it was welcoming him home.

His hand brushed against a tree, steadying himself. The bark was cold and slick, almost tender beneath his fingertips. Every nerve screamed. Every breath struggled to happen.

Still, something inside him quieted.

Not a peace, exactly but the surrender that comes when you've finally stopped pretending you're in control. He fell to one knee, pain blooming like fire through his side.

"Eva?" he whispered.

No answer came. Not in words.
Only the light, growing around him. Steady. Ghostly.

If the bride had ever existed, maybe she was here now.

Not to guide him, not to speak.

But just to bear witness.

The whispers pressed against the inside of his head, not cruel, not kind just present.

It felt like the forest was listening. Like it always has been.

James dropped fully to both knees. The light wrapped around him like a veil. The fog rose higher. His vision blurred.

His heart pounded in his chest, and with what strength he had left, he lifted his gaze.

"Please," he whispered to no one and everything. "I don't want to lose her"

The light pulsed once in reply.

And then the world went still.

He remained there, breath ragged, surrounded by an otherworldly silence that throbbed with something just out of reach. The fog swirled gently around him like breath from a sleeping giant, carrying that low, slow pulse like a heartbeat buried beneath the forest floor.

James trembled. His hands sank into the mossy ground. It was damp and spongy, as though the earth itself had softened in sympathy.

He didn't cry. He couldn't. There was only exhaustion and awe and a feeling like some part of him had been cracked open and filled with starlight.

Time was meaningless here. It might have been minutes, or hours, or something else entirely. But slowly, gently, the light began to fade not vanishing, just receding, like it had done its part.

He laid flat and still as if the sound might vanish if he moved.

That beep sharp, steady, almost digital punched through the silence like a crack in glass. It echoed between the trees, not loud, but impossible to ignore.

James blinked through the fog. His breath caught again, and not from the cold.

A scent drifted past him. Subtle. Fleeting.

But it was her. Leena.

Not the version of her wrapped in grief and distance not the one fractured by the weight of their past.

But her.

The way she smelled after a long, hot shower. When her skin was flushed and damp and clean. When she'd towel-dried her hair and curled up on the couch with his sweatshirt swallowing her frame, and the scent of lavender, warm soap, and something unmistakably her clung to the room like a spirit.

His throat clenched.

She always used the same body wash he used to tease her about it. Said she smelled like a midnight breeze and wildflowers. It was sweet and soft and sharp all at once. It clung to his pillow whenever she slept there, and even now his back in the moss, breath rattling from cracked lips, cracked ribs it twisted in the air like a phantom.

He could almost see her. Eyes tired but bright, head tilted with that half-smile she wore when she was trying not to laugh at one of his bad jokes. That playful scoff. The gentle snort that came with it.

God, her laugh.
The ache in his chest wasn't just physical anymore.
It was grief for the woman he'd lost.

For the man he'd become, and for the time they'd burned through like it was infinite.

This wasn't peace. This wasn't a reunion. This was his mind folding in on itself in its final moments scraping through every tender memory like they were film reels unraveling in slow motion.

His vision blurred again. Not from the fog. From tears.

He was dying, he really felt like it. There was no other explanation.

The pain no longer surged it simmered, low and constant, like fire banking to embers. His body had gone numb in places he didn't want to think about. The forest had swallowed him whole.

And the light the presence, the whispers they had done what they came to do.

Whatever that was.
Maybe it had always been watching.
Maybe it had been waiting.

Maybe it wanted him to remember what it was to love before it took him, before it claimed him completely.

James's lips parted, dry and trembling. "Leena…" he whispered again, and it came out cracked and barely there.

He wanted to say goodbye.

He wanted to say he was sorry.

But most of all, he wanted her to know that he still loved her. Even now. Especially now. That no matter how dark it got, she had always been the light.

Another beep cut through the quiet.
Closer this time.

Then silence.

The fog rolled forward, curling around him. The light, the ethereal glow faded to a faint glimmer, pulsing in time with something older than the stars.

And then it stopped altogether.
Like it had bowed out.
Its purpose fulfilled.
James closed his eyes.

"If this is it," he murmured, "just… let her be okay."

And in the silence that followed, he swore he heard a voice.

A echo of warmth in the cold.

He wasn't sure if it came from within or beyond.

Chapter 23

White.

Everything was white.

Not the warmth of a cloudless sky or the soft blur of snow. No, this white was sterile. Bleached. Hollow.

Leena woke.

It wasn't a gentle thing. Not like drifting up from a dream. It was clawing scraping her way out of something black and bottomless. Her lungs burned on that first breath, the air sharp with antiseptic. Her eyes squinted against fluorescent light, so bright it made her skull ache.

The ceiling didn't belong to the cabin.

She tried to move, but her arms were weighted. IVs tugged at her skin. Her fingers twitched. The beeping of a heart monitor filled the silence, slow and steady.

Then came the worst part.

She was alone.

Not in the peaceful kind of way. Not nestled under flannel in the arms of someone she trusted. An emptiness that cracked the air. That made the loneliness scream behind her ribs.

Her lips cracked as she spoke. "James?"

It was a croak. A ghost of a voice.

A nurse leaned into her vision, gentle but unfamiliar. "Hey… you're okay. You're safe."

"James," she repeated, a little louder, throat on fire.

The nurse smiled, cautiously. "He's here. Still in a coma"

Confusion struck her like a fever. "Still? He was… with me."

"In the car," the nurse said softly, thinking she understood. "Yes. You were both brought in together. You've been unconscious for nearly three weeks."

But Leena wasn't thinking of a car. Her heart pounded.

"There was a cabin," she murmured. "Woods. Mist. We were… we were together."

The nurse tilted her head slightly. "You've been dreaming, sweetheart. But it's okay. That's common. It's the brain's way of coping."

Leena shook her head barely. "Eva. Wren. The diner."

The nurse looked startled.

Before Leena could ask anything else, exhaustion overtook her again and the world began to blur, the white light swallowing her whole.

Two Days Later

This time when she woke, the light didn't hurt.

The fog in her head had thinned, though everything still moved in slow motion. Her body ached in strange, hidden places. Her skin prickled. The silence in the room was oppressive.

But her memories what she could gather, weren't of pain.

They were of rain-slicked pine trees. A fire dancing in a stone hearth. The smell of coffee, of bacon, of James' shirt wrapped around her frame. The ghost of Eva's voice. The bride. The journal. The light in the forest.

It had all felt real.

Why couldn't she remember anything else?

The door opened and a doctor stepped in. Older, kind-eyed, with a clipboard hugged to his chest.

"Leena," he said softly. "You're making progress. I wanted to come by and answer some questions. If you have them."

She blinked at him. "Why am I here?"

"You and James were in a car accident," he explained, approaching slowly. "There was a storm. An oncoming vehicle hydroplaned. Hit you both nearly head-on. Emergency crews got to you quickly."

She stared at him blankly. "Car?"

The doctor hesitated. "You don't remember?"

"No." She sat straighter, wincing. "Just… the cabin. The woods. A woman named Eva. And James. Always James."

He nodded slowly. "Sometimes trauma does this. The mind shields you from the worst. It weaves memory and imagination together to make sense of the chaos."

Leena looked away. "It felt more like the truth than this."

"Then hold onto it," he said, a little softer. "Sometimes, healing starts with believing in something."

There was a knock at the door, and a younger doctor entered with a quiet voice and a series of simple questions her name, the president, the date.

She failed more than she passed.

Then they were gone.

Later, a nurse arrived, wheeling in a machine.

"We're just going to check on something real quick," she said. "Standard, after this kind of trauma."

"What kind of scan?"

The nurse paused. "An ultrasound."

Leena frowned. "Why would I need ?"

"It's protocol," the nurse said. "But… also because we found something. It appears you're pregnant, Leena."

Her world cracked sideways.

"No," she whispered.

"We'll go slow," the nurse said gently, already applying the gel.

The screen lit up. There it was small, pulsing, undeniable.

A flicker of life.

The heartbeat thudded softly in the room. Leena could hardly breathe.

Her hand moved toward the image. Her voice shook. "When?"

"We don't know exactly yet.
The cabin. The firelight. The way James had held her that night desperate, aching.

It all surged back like floodwater.

She whispered, "It was real."

And the nurse, not understanding, just smiled and wiped her hand gently.

Alone again, Leena turned to the window, grey clouds painting the world beyond it.

She whispered into the silence.

"Please wake up, James. Please find your way home."

Her thoughts spun as the day passed in sterile stillness. Doctors filtered in and out, checking vitals, asking questions she only half-understood. They showed her scans, referenced data, murmured about head trauma and long-term recovery. But Leena wasn't listening. Not really.

All she could think about was the fire crackling in the hearth. The scent of rain on James' skin. The way he whispered, "together"

She thought of Eva. Of Wren. The aching sadness of love lost. The way Eva had waited, until the forest no longer answered.

Her hand gripped the thin blanket tighter.

James wasn't Wren.
She wasn't Eva.

They weren't going to be another tragic story the woods swallowed whole.

When the nurse returned, Leena asked again if she could see him. She begged, almost. But they said no for now. His brain activity was steady but minimal.

So she waited by the window, watching the light shift. Each second, she whispered one more prayer into the quiet.

Please find your way home.

Please remember me.

Please… don't let me raise this child alone.

And as the sky darkened, Leena finally closed her eyes.

Still believing he'd come back to her.

Because if anything from that other world had been real it was him.

Chapter 24

Darkness.

It had been so complete thick and absolute, like drowning in black water. James floated in it for what could've been minutes or centuries. There was no time in that place. No weight. No pain.

Then came the cracking light.

It split the darkness like a fault line. Thin, at first. A sliver. Then wider, forcing its way in like a sunrise through broken blinds.

Then sound.

Muffled. Distant. A chorus of things he couldn't place. A beep, steady and cold. A voice. A woman's, not Leena's. Mechanical, maybe. Talking to someone else.

James stirred. Not his body his mind.

And suddenly, pain.
It rushed in violently, as if his brain had been waiting for a signal before unleashing it all at once. His chest. His ribs. His legs. His face felt swollen. His skin ached under something rough no, not rough. Starched. Sheets. Hospital sheets.

A single word clawed its way out from the center of the chaos.

Leena.

He tried to say it, but only a wheeze escaped.

His eyelids lifted a fraction. Blurry figures moved past, shadows in a sterile white blur. There was a ceiling above him, unfamiliar and too bright. His mind grasped at fragments like shrapnel.

The forest.
Her laugh.
Blood on pines.
Eva.
The light.

A tear leaked from the corner of his eye, but he didn't feel it fall. Darkness enveloped him again

James blinked awake again, this time to less pain and more clarity. The beeping was rhythmic. So was the ache in his limbs. His body was wrapped in a blanket of dull discomfort broken, but healing.

He turned his head, slow as molasses.

A nurse noticed. "Hey there," she said softly. "Glad to see those eyes open again."

James licked his lips. It took a second

"Leena…"

No. He wasn't waiting anymore.

The ferocity the primal surge that had once driven him to tear through the woods rose again. His breath caught, and he threw the covers back with one trembling hand.

Every joint screamed. Every breath threatened collapse. But James didn't care. He ripped off the heart monitor leads, ignored the sudden alarm beeping as machines registered his disobedience.

He swung his legs over the bed. His feet hit the cold floor. He stood.

The world spun sideways.

But he stayed standing.

He stumbled forward like a man escaping a prison. IV pole clattering behind him, he shoved the door open.

A nurse shouted something maybe his name, maybe a curse but he didn't hear it clearly. An orderly came into view, arms reaching.

James pushed past them both.

"Leena," he rasped, more breath than sound.

He made it halfway down the hall.

His vision blurred.

A television mounted above the nurse's station flickered a scene from some late-night movie playing quietly. Two figures danced in a softly lit room. The woman rested her head on the man's chest. He kissed her forehead.

The screen glowed with nostalgia.

The music played gently beneath it.

It was the last thing James heard before the world tilted, went white again, and he collapsed to the floor.

The same song from the diner.

That old record.

Peggy and Cap.

And then nothing.

Darkness.

Not the kind you shut your eyes into. This was deeper. A black so complete it pressed against him from every direction thick, humid, consuming. No up. No down. No sense of time. Just pain, shifting through him in slow, tidal waves.

James floated in it.

There were flashes like dying stars moments breaking through the void. Leena's smile. Her laugh, so soft it fractured him. Her voice calling out through the woods. The heat of her skin under his fingertips. Her scent, drifting through the forest mist like something sacred like lavender and soap, and something else uniquely her, a kind of brightness that couldn't be bottled. He remembered, curling up next to him, hair damp, skin warm. That smell. That comfort.

Gone now.

The pain returned in pulses. His ribs screamed. His head throbbed. His lungs felt like they were trying to fold in on themselves.

"James," the name echoed but not in a voice he knew.

Then, light.

But not the sterile kind. Not white walls or fluorescent tubes.

No, this was soft. Ethereal. It hung in the air like mist caught in moonlight. It had weight and shape but refused to be defined. And in the middle of it her face. Not Leena's. Not Eva's. A woman from the diner.

Janet?

But it wasn't the diner anymore. Her nurse's scrubs peeked through now, replacing the retro uniform. The air smelled like antiseptic, but her smile was still warm.

James blinked.

"Good, you're still with us," she said gently. "You gave us a hell of a scare."

The light seemed to pull back. The fog in his brain thick, muddy. He tried to ask about Leena but all that came out was a low groan.

"She's okay," Janet said, answering the question before he asked it. "She's awake. She's been asking about you."

Awake.

That word hit his brain like a chime in the night. He tried to sit up, but his body rebelled, nerves sparking like a downed power line.

"You need rest. But she's just down the hall."

He didn't believe it. Couldn't. The last thing he remembered was the woods swallowing him whole. The whispering voices. The mist. The light growing bigger, swallowing everything in its path.

Was this another illusion?
A doctor appeared beside Janet, checking vitals, shining a light into his eyes. "Welcome back, James. You've been through a lot. You're in the hospital. You and Leena were in a head-on collision almost a month ago. You've been unconscious for quite some time."

"How long?" James rasped.

"Almost four weeks," the doctor said, his voice steady. "Leena woke up a few days ago. She's recovering. So are you. But it's going to take time."

James barely heard him. The world around him tilted, the bright edges of reality blurring. All he could think of was her. Her voice. Her tears. Her body curled in that old cabin bed, whispering promises into the dark.

He licked his lips again, desperate to speak, but all that came out was, "Cabin?"

Janet looked at the doctor. Then back at James. "You talked about it a lot while you were under. Something about… Wren? Eva?"

The names made his chest seize.

Had any of it been real?

The doctor scribbled something onto a chart. "Comas are strange. The mind protects itself. Constructs dreams. Stories. It's not uncommon. It's just your brain trying to cope with trauma."

But James knew. He knew.

Eva. Wren. The fog. The flickering light in the woods. It meant something.

And Leena.

She was the one constant no matter the version of the world.

He closed his eyes again, exhaustion clawing him back into sleep. But not before whispering one last thing to Janet:

"Tell her I'm here.

Chapter 25

There was shouting. A rush of white. Then black again.

But the black wasn't empty this time. It pulsed with a faint heart-beat. Somewhere, a thread held fast. A hand. A voice.

James drifted, weightless, like floating just beneath the surface of a still lake, moonlight overhead and silence stretching out around him. But he wasn't alone.

He heard her.

Faint. Like a whisper through pine.

"Come back to me."

He reached for the sound.

His eyes opened.

Everything was dim late night, maybe early morning. His throat burned. Tubes. Monitors. Pain again, but less urgent now. Familiar.

The first thing he saw… was her.

Leena.

Sitting next to him. Pale, eyes tired and red-rimmed but beautiful in a way that nearly undid him.

Her hand was curled around his, her other resting low on her belly. His gaze drifted there, then back to her eyes.

"I found my way," he croaked.

She didn't speak just launched forward, arms around his shoulders, holding him like gravity depended on it. He winced, pain flaring, but he didn't care. He held her too.

There were tears. Both of them. Messy and silent.

It was a long time before either of them found words again.

"I thought I lost you," she whispered.

"I chased you through hell," he whispered back.

She pulled away just enough to look at him, brushing hair from his forehead. "It wasn't hell. It was something else. Something… I don't know. Real. Or not. But it felt real."

He nodded. "It was."

Leena looked down at her stomach. "There's something else, James."

He followed her gaze.

"You're pregnant," he said quietly. Like he already knew.

She nodded, a tear slipping down her cheek. "They told me a few days ago. I didn't know how. Or when. Or even if it would survive everything we went through."

He stared at her in disbelief at the miracle, at the weight of everything they had endured.

"We came back with more than just memories," he said. "We brought something with us."

"You found me," he said.

"No," she whispered. "You never stopped trying."

Silence wrapped around them again. Not empty this time. Full. Heavy with things left unspoken but deeply understood.

He looked down at her belly once more. "What do we do now?"

"We heal," she said. "Really heal. And we live. For us. For them."

A small smile cracked through his pain.

The beeping of machines slowed to something steady, something human. Something real.

Outside, the first glint of dawn was breaking across the sky.

"I want to name them after the ones who waited," Leena said softly. "Eva. Or Wren."

He nodded slowly. "Yeah. I think they'd like that."

They weren't fighting ghosts.
They were building a future.
Together.

Three days passed before James could stand without the room spinning. A week before he could shuffle the length of the hospital hallway without a nurse hovering like a storm cloud. But Leena was always near reading beside him, sketching, writing in a new journal she kept tucked beneath her pillow. Every moment was quiet, but not empty.

The world outside the hospital felt distant. Fuzzy. As if it might vanish the second they turned their backs.

But Leena kept them stable.

She spoke often of the cabin the sound the wind made when it moved through the pines.

 Eva's voice in her head, not in words, but in feeling.
James listened. And remembered.

The fog. The beeps. The desperate pull to reach her before everything fell apart.

He remembered the pain.

He remembered the light.

They still weren't sure how much had been real. Or what real even meant anymore. But the baby growing inside her was proof that something more than memory had followed them back.

"Have you told anyone yet?" James asked one afternoon, fingers laced with hers as the sun cast long gold streaks across his hospital blanket.

Leena shook her head. "Only you. I want to wait until we're somewhere else. Somewhere that doesn't smell like bleach and worry."

He nodded. "Fair."

There was a knock on the door gentle, hesitant.

A young doctor stepped in with a stack of release papers. "We're almost ready to let you go," he said with a smile. "You'll need follow-ups. Rest. But i think you three will be just fine
Leena's hand tightened in his.

The doctor moved on, oblivious to the weight of his words.

Later, in the silence, James murmured, "Do you think…?"

Leena nodded. "I think Eva and Wren were never just echoes. I think we lived their grief so we wouldn't have to carry our own alone."

That night, he was discharged.

They didn't go home. Instead, they drove. Nowhere specific just away. Back roads. Gas station coffee. Windows down even when the wind stung. Leena played Fleetwood Mac softly through the stereo.

Eventually, they pulled over by an old trail head. Unmarked. Overgrown.

But James knew the feel of the place.

And Leena did too.
They sat in silence.
"We don't have to go back," he said.
"No," she replied. "But maybe we should say thank you."

They stepped out together.

Epilogue

The gravel road curled like an old ribbon through a cathedral of trees, the canopy above painted in the softest greens and golds of summer. Shafts of sunlight broke through in streaks, catching dust and memory in the air. A distant songbird trilled, fading behind the slow hum of tires crunching over stone.

From above, it could've been any stretch of forgotten countryside.

It followed the road around the bend, past where nature had begun reclaiming a rusted road sign that once pointed toward a town long lost to most maps. It glided low over wildflowers brushing against weathered fence posts, over a patchwork of old meadows and thick woods. Then there it was.

A cabin.

Not new, but lovingly maintained. A wraparound porch hugged its frame, pale smoke curling from the chimney. A pair of boots sat by the front door. A blue enamel mug rested on the porch railing.

And past that just beyond where the grass met the waterline a small wooden dock reached into the lake like an invitation.

Two figures sat near the edge.

A man with scruffy hair and soft eyes, sun on his shoulders, patient smile on his face.

A little girl, knees tucked to her chest, a small pink fishing rod wobbling in her hands.

"Like this, Daddy?" she asked, voice curious and light.

He grinned. "Just like that, peanut. Now give it a minute. Fish around here like to think things over."

She giggled. "Like Mama?"

"Exactly."

At the edge of the dock, not far from them, an easel propped up with a canvas half-finished in soft watercolors. A woman stood before it barefoot in the grass, brush in hand, sun catching the auburn strands in her hair.

Leena she was still at peace.

She stepped back from her painting, squinting toward the dock where the giggles grew louder. The light shifted as she turned her head, smile breaking slow and genuine across her face.

The girl turned too.

"Mama!" she cried, abandoning the fishing rod, sprinting down the dock on eager feet.

The woman caught her mid-leap, arms around her tight, lifting her into the air.

Sunset dipped low behind them, casting a golden fire over the lake. From above, the whole world looked wrapped in memory, in something holy and quiet.

And if you listened close enough between the wind in the trees and the hush of water you might've heard the faintest whisper:
Welcome home.